The glamorous life

The crowd pressed forward. *My* crowd. I waved to them the way I had seen my mom and dad do a million times, pausing to make eye contact with a couple of the photographers long enough to let them get a good shot. Mom always said you had to control your image.

"Right, Miss Diva," Victoria said. Her smile was a little more relaxed as she slipped her arm through mine and turned me away from the cameras. "Let's get you on that boat."

"It's a yacht," I sniffed.

She laughed, but really? I was being serious. We were about to be hosted by one of Greece's biggest movie stars, and the word *boat* didn't quite convey the appropriate glamour of the situation.

OTHER BOOKS YOU MAY ENJOY

LIGHTS, CAMERA, CASSIDY

episode two:
Paparazzi

by LINDA GERBER

PUFFIN BOOKS
An Imprint of Penguin Group (USA) Inc.

PUFFIN BOOKS

Published by the Penguin Group

Penguin Young Readers Group, 345 Hudson Street, New York, New York 10014, U.S.A.

Penguin Group (Canada), 90 Eglinton Avenue East, Suite 700, Toronto, Ontario, Canada M4P 2Y3
(a division of Pearson Penguin Canada Inc.)

Penguin Books Ltd, 80 Strand, London WC2R 0RL, England

Penguin Ireland, 25 St Stephen's Green, Dublin 2, Ireland (a division of Penguin Books Ltd)

Penguin Group (Australia), 250 Camberwell Road, Camberwell, Victoria 3124, Australia
(a division of Pearson Australia Group Pty Ltd)

Penguin Books India Pvt Ltd, 11 Community Centre,
Panchsheel Park, New Delhi - 110 017, India

Penguin Group (NZ), 67 Apollo Drive, Rosedale, Auckland 0632, New Zealand
(a division of Pearson New Zealand Ltd)

Penguin Books (South Africa) (Pty) Ltd, 24 Sturdee Avenue,
Rosebank, Johannesburg 2196, South Africa

Registered Offices: Penguin Books Ltd, 80 Strand, London WC2R 0RL, England

Published by Puffin Books, a division of Penguin Young Readers Group, 2012

1 3 5 7 9 10 8 6 4 2

LIBRARY OF CONGRESS CATALOGING-IN-PUBLICATION DATA IS AVAILABLE

Puffin Books ISBN 978-0-14-241815-4

Interior designed by Theresa Evangelista
Text set in Adobe Caslon regular

Printed in the United States of America

For Jenna, my Greek Adventure companion

Acknowledgments: Many thanks to my agent, Elaine Spencer; my ever-patient editor, Kristin Gilson; cover designer extraordinaire Theresa Evangelista; and my new Greek friend Popi Papazoglou. I couldn't have done it without you.

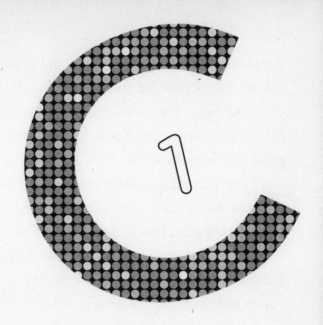

A sign on the wall in the Athens

airport said, GREECE WELCOMES A NEW MYTH. YOURS.

I had to stop and take a picture of it because it fit my situation so well. Arriving in Greece, I felt like I was actually stepping into an adventure of mythical proportions.

My mom and dad host a popular television travel show called *When in Rome*, and I've been all over the world with them, but this was the first time I was traveling on my own. Or at least without them. I did have my tutor, Victoria, with me. It was the only way they would let me go. And by "only way," I mean it was one of a long list of rules and conditions.

My mom and dad's network had invited me to help host a travel special on Greece that would air on their sister kids' network. The only problem was, my mom and dad's show was already scheduled to shoot in Papua, New Guinea, at the same time. They wouldn't have even considered letting me do the Greece special if it wasn't for Victoria. And a good deal of pressure from the network.

They wanted to cash in on the surge of publicity *When in Rome* had gotten since our recent visit to Spain. Without intending to, I had landed myself in trouble there, and landed on the front pages of the tabloids in the process. The attention got a little too intense, so my mom and dad sent me to stay with my gramma in Ohio to get me out of the spotlight and let things settle down.

It didn't work. Newspaper and television reporters swarmed Gramma's farm. I probably did more interviews in the few weeks I was there than my mom and dad did in a year. Our executive director, Cavin, insisted that they should take advantage of my name recognition instead of hiding me away. Finally, my mom and dad gave in when I was invited to do the special.

Thinking about Cavin made me think about his son, Logan, and that made my stomach flip. At one time, Logan had been my best friend. When we were kids, he used to travel on location with the show just like I did. We hung out together all the time. And then Logan's mom made him go back to live with her in Ireland. I didn't see him for over two years, until—without any warning—he came back to the show when we were in Spain.

And I realized I liked him.

I mean, really *liked* him.

And the way he came looking for me before he left Spain, I had a feeling that he liked me, too.

We'd been meeting online to chat as often as we could since then, and things had just started to get interesting when I was invited to come to Greece.

I closed my eyes and remembered Logan's smile. His green eyes, fringed with black lashes. His Irish accent and the way he let his words lilt up at the end of a sentence. I sighed.

"Are you feeling quite all right?" Victoria asked.

By then we were standing in the long immigration line, waiting to be processed.

"I'm good," I told her, even though my stomach felt like it had been inhabited by a vicious breed of attack butter-flies. *Excitement*, I told myself, even though I knew it was much more than that.

If I ever wanted to return to my parents' show—and be with Logan again—I had to prove to them that I could keep out of trouble. That I could be an asset. A lot was riding on this trip. What if I wasn't up to the challenge?

Suddenly, I felt claustrophobic in the long line of people. Like I couldn't breathe.

"Actually," I told Victoria, "I think I need to go to the restroom." Anywhere to get away from the crowd for a moment. I had to pull myself together.

She glanced at her watch. "Can it wait until we get to baggage claim? The producers said they would be sending a driver to pick us up, and I'm afraid we'll keep him waiting if we lose our place in line now."

"You stay," I said. "Save our spot. I'll be right back." I didn't wait for her to say no, but sprinted to the nearest bathroom.

You are la chica moda, I told my image in the mirror. *You can do this.*

La chica moda, in case you didn't know, is the nickname the tabloids in Spain gave me. It means "the fashionable girl." And I swear, it's not something I thought a whole lot about before Spain. Fashion, I mean. I just wore what I liked. But since I pick up clothes from all over the world and have developed what the papers called my own "sense of style," they seemed to think it was newsworthy. Once I was already in the news, that is.

That kind of a nickname can become a burden. I mean, it's a lot to live up to, right? I try not to think about it, but it's there in the back of my mind, ready to pounce whenever my confidence slips.

Of course, my mom's quick tutorial on how to behave like a television personality didn't help much. "You never know when someone will be watching," she told me before I left for Greece. "Or when your picture might be taken. Remember that whenever we are in the public eye, we are always *on*."

Thanks so much, Mom. Way to make me perpetually self-conscious.

I splashed my face with water and stared at myself in the mirror. I hardly even recognized the girl who stared back. My eyes looked bluer that usual. Bright, eager. My cheeks flushed pink with anticipation. I usually straightened my blonde hair, but I'd left my straightener at home this trip on the advice of the makeup guy with my mom and dad's show.

"You've got naturally wavy hair," Daniel had said. "You don't want to fight the humidity in Greece by trying to straighten it all the time. Remember, natural is your friend."

Taking a deep breath, I repeated the affirmations that had been my mantra from the moment I left Cleveland. I could show my mom and dad. I could be *on*. I could be a star. I set my sunglasses on top of my head and tossed my natural waves and stared down the girl in the mirror. "Let's do this thing."

I saw the sign with my name on it the minute we rolled our luggage out of the customs area. It's the first time I've seen a driver holding up *my* name. Usually, it's my mom's or dad's name on the placard. A little thrill rippled through me and I nudged Victoria. "Look!" I whispered.

Holding the sign was a tall man in a black suit and a crisp white shirt. He had dark, wavy hair and even darker eyes that watched the passengers coming through the entry.

Our driver, I guessed. He must have recognized me—or at least saw the way I reacted to the sign he was holding—because he tucked the sign under his arm and waved us over.

"Miss Cassidy, Miss Victoria," he said. "I am Magus Demetriou. *Kalos irthate stin Ellada.* Welcome to Greece." His voice was big and deep, just like he was. Seriously. Besides being tall, the guy had thick, wide shoulders and a solid-looking build beneath his suit. He looked more like a bodyguard than a driver.

"Mr. Kouropoulos asked that I bring you to the yacht directly," he said, giving a little nod first to me, and then to Victoria.

Oh, did I mention that part of the deal with the travel special was that we would be sailing around the Greek islands on a movie star's yacht? Yeah. It's a rough life, but I'm willing to make the sacrifice.

"Is it far to the harbor?" I asked.

"Perhaps far for some, not so far for others." He smiled in a way that made me wonder if he was joking or giving me some kind of riddle or what.

Which meant I had no idea how to respond. All I could come up with was, "Oh," and that didn't quite have the star quality I was going for.

But then, he probably didn't even hear the answer anyway. He was already in motion, taking the luggage cart from Victoria and motioning with his head for us to follow him.

"I trust your flight was pleasant?" he said over his shoulder.

"It was really nice," I said. "Thank you."

He led us outside through a pair of sliding-glass doors. I squinted in the bright Mediterranean sunshine and pulled the sunglasses off the top of my head, but stopped short of putting them on. Right in front of us, a sleek white limousine with tinted-glass windows idled near the loading-zone curb. I barely had time to wonder if some big celebrity was flying into Athens that afternoon before Magus stepped up to pay the uniformed attendant and I realized the limo was for us. Niiice.

We sometimes got limousine service when I traveled with my mom and dad, but I wasn't expecting it for just me. Well, me and Victoria. I settled the sunglasses onto my nose and slipped my cell phone from my pocket to take a quick picture to post on my blog. And to show Logan how the network was rolling out the red carpet for this show. Not bad for my first gig.

The attendant scurried to load our luggage into the trunk of the limousine while Magus opened the backseat door for Victoria and me. I slid gracefully onto the cool, buttery-soft leather seats inside, *feeling* like a star. Now all I had to do for the next week and a half was *act* like one.

"Miss Cassidy," Magus said as we wove slowly through the traffic surrounding the city, "You asked how long it would take to reach the port. As you can see, it could be a while, by the clock."

I leaned forward in my seat to hear him better. "You said it could be long for some, and not so long for others. What did you mean?"

"Ah. You were listening. Are you a student of philosophy, Miss Cassidy?"

Victoria leaned forward then, too. If there was anything she loved, it was a "teaching moment." It sounded like she and Magus were made from the same mold. "Philosophy," Victoria told me, "means 'love of wisdom.' A good many of the world's great philosophers were Greek."

"That is right," Magus said, pleased. "Philosophy teaches us how to look at the world and find truth. In this instance, we see that we are stuck in traffic. Does this make our journey longer?"

His eyes met mine in the rearview mirror as he waited for my answer. "Not if you're talking about distance," I said. "I'm guessing it takes more time, though."

"But what is time?" he asked.

Again, he waited for an answer. "Um. I don't know?"

"Protagoras tells us that man is the measure of all things. Do you know what this means?"

When I didn't answer, Victoria chimed in. "Things are as we say they are."

"So . . ." I said, trying to follow the logic. "If I say the trip is long, it's long, and if I say it's short, it's short—even if it takes the same hour either way?" You tell me. Does that make any sense? I didn't think so.

But Magus said, "Yes."

And Victoria said, "Exactly."

And I wondered if philosophy was like one of those jokes that wasn't supposed to make sense, but people laughed anyway.

However you looked at it, before too long, we reached the port. I watched through the window for a glimpse of the yacht as the limousine rolled to a stop.

"Oh, my gosh," I breathed. "Look at that."

Victoria leaned over to look out my side. She didn't say anything, but I could feel her next to me as she suddenly went rigid—not on account of the yacht, but because of what stood between us and the yacht.

On the dock, maybe two dozen people shouted and pushed and waved at us from behind sawhorse barricades. A couple of burly-looking security guards were holding them back or I'm pretty sure they would have rushed the limousine.

Victoria tapped Magus on the shoulder. "What is all this?" she asked. Her voice had gone as stiff as her posture.

Magus shrugged one huge shoulder. "Not to worry; they simply wish to see you." He killed the engine and un-buckled his seat belt.

I realized how well the limousine's soundproofing

worked when he pushed his door open, and voices swirled in with the clean saltwater smell of the sea.

"It's her!"

"Miss Barnett!"

"Over here!"

Magus climbed out of the car and closed his door firmly behind him, muffling the words once more.

I watched the crowd for a moment, then turned to Victoria, practically bouncing in my seat. "Can you believe all these people are here to see me?"

"Well, of course," she said drily. "You are quite a star." She smiled when she said it, but I didn't miss the way she watched out the window. Guarded. Wary. And I had a pretty good idea I knew why.

Victoria and I had been stalked by some aggressive paparazzi in Spain. She was probably thinking about how they chased us through the streets of Valencia, right into the lobby of our hotel. But this was different. There were barricades. Guards holding the paparazzi back. And besides, it's not like they were going to be able to chase after us as we got onto the yacht.

When Magus opened the back door for us, the voices rushed in again. Calling my name. Calling for *me*. I forgot all about Victoria and her hesitation and stepped out into the warmth of sunlight and admiration.

The crowd pressed forward. *My* crowd. I waved to them

the way I had seen my mom and dad do a million times, pausing to make eye contact with a couple of the photographers long enough to let them get a good shot. Mom always said you had to control your image.

"Right, Miss Diva," Victoria said. Her smile was a little more relaxed as she slipped her arm through mine and turned me away from the cameras. "Let's get you on that boat."

"It's a yacht," I sniffed.

She laughed, but really? I was being serious. We were about to be hosted by one of Greece's biggest movie stars, and the word *boat* didn't quite convey the appropriate glamour of the situation. Besides, even *yacht* was an understatement for the *Pandora*. She was practically a ship, long and sleek and glistening white against a backdrop of cobalt-blue water. Her name was painted in both Greek and Roman lettering on the bow. A crimson-carpeted gangplank stretched up from the pier to the deck. (Ha. I was right about rolling out the red carpet.) As soon as our backs were turned to the paparazzi, I snuck a quick photo of the *Pandora* for my blog.

My heart skipped a beat as I let my eyes follow the gangplank's path to where our movie-star host and his son were waiting to greet us. I'd seen pictures of both of them online, but none of the photos even came close to the real thing.

Nikos Kouropolous—who, from what I had read in his

online bio, was only about five months older than me—had heavy Mediterranean brows and thick, dark hair, his short curls ruffling in the breeze.

His father, Constantine Kouropoulos, probably once had the same dark curls as Nikos, but now his hair was streaked with silver. He wore it brushed straight back from his forehead. Very cosmopolitan, even if I thought it was a little severe.

But I wasn't exactly giving Mr. Kouropolos or his hair much thought at that moment. I poked Victoria. "That's him!" I whispered. "That's Nikos."

2

From all I'd learned about him,
Nikos Kouropoulos and I were a lot alike. My mom and
dad were famous television personalities, and his dad was
a famous actor. We both grew up one step away from the
spotlight. That's probably why the network chose the two
of us to host their first-ever kids' travel special. Of course, it
probably didn't hurt that his dad had offered the use of his
yacht for the show.

Whatever the reason, I was excited to become friends
with Nikos. And to prove to my mom and dad that I could
do just fine on the road—or the sea. After the (pretty huge)
mistakes I'd made in Spain, I had a lot of proving to do if I
was going to convince them to let me travel with them again.

● ● ● ● ●

Travel tip: Greeks are known for being warm and hospitable. When meeting someone for the first time, smile and maintain direct eye contact.

I was very aware of all eyes on Victoria and me as we walked up the gangplank toward the yacht. The paparazzi on the pier were still calling my name, but I could barely hear them anymore. Their little cameras were nothing compared to the two production cameras pointed at us from aboard the yacht. I'm talking serious movie cameras. One of them was on an aerial lift, the cameraman hovering over the water as he filmed us from the side, and the other was mounted on some kind of dolly that rolled smoothly along the deck, following our progress.

"Wow," I whispered to Victoria. "Our equipment looks amateur compared to these things." My mom and dad's crew did have one mounted camera they used for some of the food segments of their show, but most of the footage was filmed with standard on-the-shoulder models. My dad would have killed for the kind of budget this crew must have had.

Meanwhile, no one had warned me they would be filming us before I had a chance to clean up from the flight, especially with equipment like that. Those things could pick up every zit or hair out of place. I suddenly missed our makeup guy, Daniel. He wouldn't have let them shoot a frame without a quick powder and a spritz. But I had to be *on*, and that meant I didn't get to let little things like airplane hair or super-ultra-mega high-definition cameras bother me. I had to smile and act like I had all the confidence in the world. Even when I didn't.

Nikos was the first one to greet us when we reached the top of the gangplank. *"Yiasou,"* he said. "Hello. Welcome to Greece."

His warm smile was echoed in his dark chocolate eyes so that when he looked at me, I immediately felt like I was the most important thing in his world. I could see why the fan pages called him the Greek Romeo. Of course, after the things that had been made up about me in Spain, I also knew better than to believe everything I read in the tabloids.

"Hayro pohlee," I answered, probably butchering the pronunciation. It meant "nice to meet you" and was about the only Greek phrase I'd had time to learn for the trip.

Mr. Kouropoulos clapped his hands. "Very good!" I reluctantly pulled my attention from Nikos to thank him. Up close it was obvious *he'd* had time to sit in the makeup chair, judging from the matte finish to his skin, and the powder that had settled into the fine lines around his eyes. The lines were the only thing about him that looked old, though. Like Nikos, the rest of his olive skin was smooth and his teeth were impossibly white. But unlike Nikos, his broad smile didn't quite reach his eyes. In fact, something about his eyes made me want to shiver.

My own smile froze for an instant. I looked to Victoria

in confusion, but just then one of the photographers on the pier called out to Mr. Kouropolous and suddenly his eyes lost their coldness. He turned and waved with such an easy smile, I wondered if I'd been imagining things.

Like . . . had he started to turn toward the paparazzi half a breath before we heard the shout?

And . . . did Nikos flinch just a little when his dad patted him on the back?

I didn't have much time to consider either question. Because just then, Nikos grabbed my hand and pulled me over to the railing next to him and his dad. He lifted our joined hands in the air, and he waved at the cameras on the pier with his other hand.

I forgot about whatever weird vibe I thought I had felt and decided just to enjoy the moment. Following Nikos's lead, I posed and waved and pulled out my Miss America smile, and I might even have started blowing kisses if Victoria hadn't cleared her throat behind me.

I shot her a look and she shot me one right back, mouthing that I should tone it down a little. I rolled my eyes. Please. I wasn't hamming it up *that* much.

But then Victoria signaled me with a nod of her head, pointing out a woman on the deck I hadn't noticed before. She was speaking into a headset microphone, consulting the clipboard in her hand, and pointing here and there with little stabs of her finger. The director, I guessed. Another thing not like *When in Rome*. Our director never micro-managed the shoots the way it looked like she was doing. He'd tell everyone what he wanted and then stand back and let them do it. But then, she didn't look like the type who would leave that much out of her control.

This lady had *uptight* written all over her, from her blunt-cut no-nonsense hairdo to her man-tailored white linen suit. Plus, the way she pursed her lips together was so—uh-oh.

Uptight Director Lady glanced up and noticed I was watching her. She made a face that looked like a cross between a grimace and a snarl and yanked off her headset. "Cut!"

She stalked toward me, brushing past Victoria like she wasn't even there. "Cassidy, darling," the woman said with a tone that made me feel anything but darling, "you're new to this, so let me explain. When we do the rehearsed segments, I'll want you to pay attention to me, but for the candid shots, you are to pretend I'm not here. Pretend *we're* not here." She pointed to the camera on the dolly and then back to herself. "Can you do that, sweetheart?"

I wanted to tell her that I wasn't her sweetheart and I wasn't "new to this." I grew up around a television crew. Maybe not in front of the camera the whole time, but still. I knew how things were done—at least with my mom and dad's show.

Of course, different crews had different ways of doing things, and if I was going to show my mom and dad I could be a professional, I had to get used to that. So I nodded and apologized.

"Hmmm." She gave me the up-and-down in a way that made me feel very small and un–TV starish. I was trying to think of something to say to lighten the moment when Victoria came to my rescue.

She reached out to shake the director's hand. "You must be CJ," she said. "I'm Victoria Chen, Miss Barnett's tutor. John Pareo from the network said I should speak to you about her lesson schedule."

For a heartbeat, I thought CJ wasn't going to answer Victoria, judging by the snotty way she was looking at her. But then she said, "Of course. We will be going over the agenda and procedures with Mr. Kouropolous and the children shortly. You're welcome to join us."

Victoria managed to keep her smile from slipping, even though I'm sure she didn't like being invited to a planning meeting as an afterthought any more than I liked being called a child. "I would appreciate that," she said. "Thank you."

CJ didn't even acknowledge Victoria's thanks, but turned to the guys with the cameras and the microphones and yelled, "That's it for now. Set up for the harbor shots and we'll reconvene at one."

Once the cameras had been turned off, Mr. Kouropoulos abandoned the railing. "We are very pleased to have you with us," he said to Victoria and me. "I hope this experience will be both profitable and enjoyable."

Profitable wasn't something I usually thought much about, although I did suppose if this trip wasn't meant to be profitable, the network wouldn't have sent me. "Thank you," I said sincerely.

"Come," Nikos said, "I will show you to the salon." He held out his arm like he was going to escort me into a dance or something. His smile was very charming, but the arm thing didn't look like a natural move for him.

Nikos's dad watched intently, and I supposed he was the one who choreographed the scene. Parents can be kind of awkward sometimes.

"Oh. Thank you." I slipped my hand around the crook of his elbow, hoping that was what I was supposed to do.

He led me—somewhat stiffly—into a huge room that was lined with windows on three sides. The polished wood floor and all the brass fixtures gleamed softly in the light. A collection of white couches and chairs were arranged among bookcases; tall, sprawling plants; and end tables. There was even a mahogany baby grand piano in the corner.

"Wow. This is really nice," I told Nikos.

"We try," he said drily.

Mr. Kouropoulos's cell phone rang and he excused himself to answer it. Whatever the person on the other end of the line said to him didn't make him happy. Not that I was trying to watch him, but it was kind of hard to miss the tone of his voice and the way he gestured angrily as he replied.

The rest of us stood there awkwardly until Victoria discreetly suggested we take a seat. And just in time, too, because just then, CJ blustered into the room, followed by one of the crew members.

CJ snapped her fingers like she was summoning a waiter, and the assistant handed her her clipboard and a pencil. She took them both without a word and then waved Mr. Kouropoulos over.

He abruptly ended his phone call and stalked back to the chairs, but by the time he settled into his seat, he was all smiles and charm again. "Now where were we?"

CJ pulled a small stack of papers from the clipboard and passed a few sheets to each one of us. I shuffled through them to see our itinerary as well as a copy of the bylaws the network had sent along with my contract earlier.

"We have a lot to accomplish in our short ten days together," she said, "so please pay attention. You will notice the days are broken down into rather small chunks. This is to ensure your offscreen time as well as your schooltime each day."

I studied the page and noticed the way each day was divided. No more than four hours of work per day . . . and no less than three hours of schoolwork. My mom and dad had explained the regulations to me when they filled out all the paperwork and permission forms. I slid a quick glance at Nikos. Would he be required to do schoolwork as well? Or was that an American regulation?

He glanced up at that moment and caught me looking at him. He waggled his eyebrows at me. Give me a break. I rolled my eyes back at him, and he laughed.

"Nikos!" his dad said. That's all. Just one word. But it sucked all the joy right out of Nikos. His shoulders drooped, caving inward as if he was a parade balloon and someone had just let too much air out of him.

I watched him for a moment, hoping he'd look up, hoping we'd make eye contact again so I could let him know I was sorry. That confrontation wouldn't have just happened if it weren't for me.

"Cassidy?" Victoria nudged me gently. Another one-word reminder, but hers felt so much different. I turned back to my itinerary.

"We will dock in Mykonos early this evening and over-night at port," CJ continued. "In the morning, we will take the smaller boat to Delos, where we'll begin shooting the first segment." She glanced up at me sharply. "I trust you've memorized your lines?"

I nodded. My mom had made me recite them to her before she even signed all the papers to let me come. I peeked over at Nikos to see if he'd learned his lines as well, but he didn't look as if he was even listening.

"The next few days," CJ said, "are earmarked for wrapping up the segment and sailing throughout the Cyclades islands. If we need to take more time filming in Delos, you will have less time for recreation on those days."

"What kind of recreation?" I asked.

"You will be responsible for your own downtime."

Nikos perked up. So he was listening after all. "Some of the islands have great beaches," he told me. "There is swimming, snorkeling, wakeboarding. . . ."

CJ cleared her throat. "May we continue?" She slowly and painfully outlined the rest of the shoots. We'd have six on-location shoots and two days at sea to get onboard shots. Which I already knew since I'd been over my copy of the itinerary, like, a million times since I got it. But maybe CJ needed to go over everything anyway, just to make sure we all understood what we were supposed to be doing. At least that much felt familiar. Our executive director did the same thing at the beginning of the shoots for *When in Rome*.

Our executive director. Cavin. Logan's dad. Another lonely pang twisted in my stomach. How much longer until I could talk to Logan?

Beneath the table, I snuck my cell phone from my pocket and leaned back just enough so I could see the time display. One o'clock in the afternoon. Papua was eight hours ahead of Greece, which meant where Logan was, it was already nine at night. We had agreed to sign in if we could at ten his time. Another hour. I sighed.

I don't know if she noticed me checking my phone or not, but CJ finally stopped talking. "You must be tired," she said, even though there was no sympathy in the tone of her voice. She straightened her papers and shoved them back under the metal claw on her clipboard. "Why don't you go get rested and cleaned up and we'll reconvene at three for lunch." And with that, she turned and walked off.

Part of me was happy to be released, but the bigger part of me worried that I might have just offended her, which wouldn't be good for convincing the network—and my parents—I was ready to be on camera.

"Thanks!" I called after her.

She didn't turn around.

"You'll want to see your cabins," Mr. Kouropolous said. Nikos started to stand, but his dad shook his head and Nikos dropped back into his chair, frowning. "Zoe!" Mr. Kouropoulos called.

A girl with really pretty, long, wavy, black hair, wearing a white uniform, appeared out of nowhere (well, obviously she was *somewhere* nearby when he called her, but I hadn't seen her before). She did a kind of half curtsy and said, "Yes, sir!"

"Could you please show our guests to their rooms?"

Zoe bobbed her head in turn to Victoria and me. "You come with me, please." She said each word with the kind of slow, careful enunciation that came with speaking a foreign language. I knew that kind of hesitancy well; it sounded like me every time we visited another country.

What was the working age in Greece? I wondered. Zoe didn't look like she could be much older than me. She was about my height, and had big, brown eyes and long, black eyelashes that curled up at the tips the way I tried to make mine do with mascara but pretty much failed.

"Please, this way." She gestured for us to follow her and led us down a short flight of steps into a wide, carpeted hallway the next level down.

"She's a beautiful yacht," Victoria said.

Zoe's fingers trailed lightly, almost lovingly, along the handrail. "Yes, she is."

"Have you sailed with her often?" Victoria asked.

"Oh." Zoe looked unsure, but said, "Yes." She paused for a moment to pull open a glass-and-brass door that led to a narrower, but still-spacious corridor. "Your cabins are this way, please," she said softly.

The walls of the corridor were paneled in some kind of deep-colored wood, with beveled glass sconces spaced about every three feet so that it didn't seem dark at all. There were maybe five or six gleaming wooden doors along the corridor. Zoe stopped in front of one with a brass plate on it that read, GALENE.

"Oh, look." Victoria turned to me. "Our room is named for a sea nymph."

"Your room," Zoe corrected, and swung the door open wide. "Miss Cassidy will stay across the hall." She pointed to another door with the name DIONE on its brass plate.

Okay, that was weird. Not the name on the door or the fact that I got my own room when Victoria's looked plenty big for the both of us—I liked that part. But having someone (presumably) my own age calling me 'miss'? That was just too much. "You can just call me Cassidy," I said.

Zoe nodded slowly, as if she had to turn the request over in her mind. "This way . . . Cassidy."

3

The first thing I noticed as I walked

into my cabin was the size. I always imagined that cabins on yachts would be small because, well, they were on most boats I had been on. But this room was huge.

A king-size bed sprawled near one wall, framed by sheer white curtains that draped down from the ceiling. An intricately carved desk sat at an angle in the middle of the room, behind a cushy white sofa that was scattered with gold and blue pillows.

A row of built-in shelves, drawers, and cupboards ran the entire length of the wall opposite the bed. The wall at the far end of the cabin wasn't a wall at all, but a row of windows and sliding doors that led out to a private balcony.

The second thing I noticed about my cabin was my grampa's picture propped up on the desk. And my laptop next to that. And my string of lights, winding around the doorway. And my little brass incense burner, sitting on the nightstand, its sweet-smelling smoke gently curling up into the air. It took me a second to realize what it all meant: Someone had unpacked my suitcase for me. I wasn't used to that.

"Everything is okay?" Zoe asked.

"What? Oh, yes." I took just a few steps into the room. "It's beautiful."

"Here is your bath," she said, sliding open a door beside us.

I peeked around her to see a marble-tiled bathroom with what looked like a Jacuzzi tub in the corner. A gold-framed mirror hung above a bowl sink that was set into a shiny black granite counter. Nice.

"You have everything you need?"

"Yes," I said. "This is perfect."

She started to leave, but I stopped her.

"Zoe, wait." I didn't really need anything, but I didn't want her to go yet. It had been forever since I'd had another girl my age around to talk to. Well, kind of talk to. "I . . . um . . . how do you say 'thank you' in Greek?"

She hesitated for a second, as if she didn't understand what I was asking—or why. But then she smiled, and her entire face changed. If at all possible, she was even prettier than before, and she looked more like . . . well, like someone I would hang out with. "It is *efharistoh*," she told me.

"*Efharistoh,*" I repeated.

"Yes. Very good."

"*Efharistoh*, Zoe."

"*Parakalo,*" she said. "This mean 'you are welcome.'"

She backed out of the room, and I let her go this time. I hoped that in the ten days we had on the yacht, we'd get beyond translating words.

There were still forty minutes left before I was supposed to meet Logan online, so I took a quick shower and washed off the greasy, grungy feel of travel. Wrapping up in the soft, white, terry-cloth robe (with the name PANDORA embroidered on the front in gold thread) I padded out to the main room for clean clothes, towel-drying my hair on the way. It wasn't until I was halfway across the room that I remembered—someone had unpacked my things for me.

I rushed to the wall of built-ins and yanked open a couple of drawers. There were my clothes, folded into neat little piles. Which meant . . . I pulled open another drawer and wanted to die on the spot. There lay my bras. My padded, push-up, pretend-you-have-cleavage bras I bought special for the trip. Perfect. Whoever unpacked my bags—I assumed it was Zoe—knew I was a padder.

I grabbed my clothes and plodded back into the bathroom to get dressed.

I had just pulled on my shirt when the vibration from the engines began to hum beneath my feet. We were leaving the port. I hurried out the sliding doors to the balcony to see. Below, the blue-green water churned white, foam bubbling up beneath the hull. The pier began to slip slowly away.

It was like magic, watching the shoreline stretch out behind us, all whitewashed walls and steep, green hillsides. I leaned on the railing and listened to the rush of the water beneath the yacht, felt the warm sea breeze blow through my hair. I couldn't wait to start filming the special. I'd show my mom and dad. I could go on location just as well as they could. In such a beautiful setting, I thought, nothing could possibly go wrong.

Shows what I know.

By the time I wandered back into my cabin from the balcony, I realized I had only five minutes before it was time to chat online with Logan. I hurried into the bathroom and scrunched gel into my hair, letting it fall into natural waves like Daniel suggested.

My phone chirped, letting me know It Was Time. I forgot about my hair and rushed to the desk to turn on my computer. When I opened the browser, though, nothing happened. My heart dropped. What if the connection wouldn't go through? I was on a yacht, after all. What if their satellite wasn't strong enough? What if their bandwidth was too small? What if—

But then, all the little connectivity bars at the top corner of my computer screen lit up. I was so relieved, I felt like dancing. But I wasn't online yet. Holding my breath, I typed in the username and password I found on the little instruction card on my desk.

Yes! It worked. Now for the big question . . . would Logan be on? Anticipation built as I logged on to the chat site, but then fell when I saw that his icon was dark.

It's okay, I told myself. *He's in a different time zone. Maybe he counted the hours forward instead of backward for Greece. Maybe I counted wrong.*

Opening up a new tab, I checked the world time clock website to be sure I figured the difference right. I had. Back to the first tab, I checked Logan's status again. Still dark. Disappointment opened up like a black hole right in the center of my chest, just like it did whenever I signed on and he wasn't there. I knew he couldn't always make it. *I* couldn't always make it. But it didn't make the letdown any easier.

But then I noticed a message in my chat site mailbox. From Logan. I quickly clicked on it.

**Cass—out of apt tonight sign in latr 10 ur time
Logan**

Ten at night or ten in the morning? I hoped he meant night, because at ten in the morning, I'd be off filming on Delos, and I wouldn't get to talk to him. On the other hand, ten at night would make it six in the morning for Logan, and he wasn't much of a morning person. . . .

I figured I'd find out when I signed in that night and saw if he was there or not. I grabbed my phone and reset the alarm to our new (I hoped) chat time.

Meanwhile, I still had almost an hour before lunch so I decided to upload the pictures of the limo and the yacht to my blog. At least it would give me something to do that didn't involve wondering when I would get to talk to Logan.

The blog is something I started when my grampa got sick a couple of years ago. Since he had gotten too weak to go anywhere outside the farm, I wanted to share my travels with him. After he died, I couldn't bring myself to stop posting. What had started as a way to keep me with him turned out to be a way to keep him with me. As long as I kept talking to my grampa, he wasn't really gone. At least that's what I told myself.

To the network, my blog was something else completely. They noticed how many people were starting to read the things I posted, and they decided it could be useful to my mom and dad's show. They gave me a dedicated spot on the *When in Rome* website and started keeping stats and charting demographics and all sorts of other stuff I didn't understand. I didn't like how commercial they were making it, but I couldn't really complain too much. If they didn't care about my blog, I wouldn't be on a yacht in the Aegean Sea, starring in a television special, and working my way back to *When in Rome*.

In fact, one of the many conditions for me coming to do the special was that I blog about it every day—giving a "behind the scenes" look at the show that the network could use for advance promotion.

I uploaded the photos and lost myself cropping and adjusting them so that they'd look good online. By the time I had them ready to post, it was already 2:45. Almost lunchtime. And I wasn't ready.

If CJ and crew filmed Victoria and me walking onto the yacht, they'd for sure have the cameras rolling for lunch. I wanted to look decent for at least one of the candids.

Back in the bathroom, I checked my makeup and shook my hair and tried to think of every camera angle imaginable and how each one would look on-screen. I seriously wasn't trying to be vain, but when the papers call you *la chica moda*, you'd be amazed at how many people search for any little flaw to prove you're not.

With that in mind, I had chosen to go simple for the lunch, in a powder-blue top and a pair of jeans. Not too dressy, but with a pair of beaded sandals and the sparkle of my charm necklace, not too casual, either.

I practiced my TV-star smile in the mirror. My mouth

gleamed. Or, rather, the wire of my palate expander gleamed. My smile faded as I remembered Daniel warning me about how it could catch the light on camera. I quickly spit out my appliance and rinsed it off. I had just snapped it into its storage case when I heard a timid knock on my cabin door.

"Coming!" I called.

Quickly checking myself over once more, I turned toward the door. Paused. Automatically reached up to run my fingers over the good-luck charm necklace my grampa had given me years ago. *Here we go.* I told myself. *It's showtime.*

Zoe was waiting in the hallway with Victoria. She bobbed her head as I joined them. "You are hungry?" she asked.

I actually was. I'd been too excited and nervous to eat that morning. "Yes," I said. "What are we having?"

"My mother, she makes the food," Zoe said. "You will like it."

Ah. So Zoe's mom worked on the yacht, too. Maybe that was how Zoe got her job.

She led us to the opposite end of the hallway from where we had come down earlier that afternoon. Instead of a stairwell, she paused at a set of small, ornate doors and pressed a button on the wall.

"No way," I said. "This place has an elevator!"

"What did you think of your room?" Victoria asked. "Is this place swanky or what?"

"What's 'swanky'?"

"Posh," Victoria said. "Richly furnished. Opulent."

"Are those vocabulary words?" I asked. "Do I have to know them?"

She made a big show of rolling her eyes. "No, Cassidy. You do not *have* to know the words, though it wouldn't hurt you to expand your vocabulary."

I was about to say something about giving me a break from lessons when the elevator chimed softly and the doors glided open. Zoe stood back and ushered us inside, then she followed us in and pressed the number Four button. The doors slid shut again.

"This yacht has four levels!" I whispered to Victoria.

"Five," Zoe said proudly.

I'd never been on a yacht that big before. In fact, the only time I could remember being on any yacht was when I was nine, and that one had only a single deck.

The elevator chimed once more, and the doors slid back to show a shaded deck featuring a round, white-draped dining table and a killer view. Beyond the railings, deep blue stretched out all around us, dotted by rocky islands in the distance. I could barely breathe as I stepped off the elevator. It was like I was walking into a dream.

Zoe watched me the way my gramma does when she gives me a present and she can't wait to see how much I like it.

"It's so beautiful," I breathed.

"This place is my favorite." She spread her arms wide and turned in a circle. "The most high deck on the *Pandora*."

"You know the yacht well," I said.

A cloud of something I didn't understand crossed her face. "Yes," she said simply. "I do."

There was a touch of pride in her statement, but something else, too. It felt like sadness. But why? I would like to have talked to her more to find out, but just then Mr. Kouropoulos made his grand entrance, all smiles and charm.

"Ah, there you are!" He brushed right past Zoe, making a big fuss over Victoria and me. Not so charming. Then he kissed each of us on the cheeks as if he hadn't seen us just a couple of hours before. "You look lovely, both of you."

The overenthusiastic greeting shocked me so much I started to pull back . . . until I realized the cameras must already be rolling. I'd half noticed CJ and her crew when we first stepped out onto the deck, but I'd been so distracted by the view that I hadn't given them much thought. Now I took a quick look around (careful not to let my eyes rest directly on CJ so I wouldn't get yelled at again) to see what else I had missed.

I was pleasantly surprised to find Magus standing in the corner, feet shoulder-width apart, huge hands clasped in front, dark glasses hiding his eyes. He looked very body-guard-ish. Ha. I was right.

Nikos was sitting on one of the lounge chairs nearby, bent over a cell phone. Texting, I guessed, the way his thumbs raced across the phone's keypad. He looked cute, in a Mediterranean/preppy sort of way. He had also changed during the break and now wore a crisp, white shirt and khaki trousers. He'd also stuck a pair of D&G sunglasses on top of his head and had even popped his collar. I did have to admit that the white looked good on him, with his olive skin and dark hair.

He must have sensed I was watching him because he glanced up and caught me looking. Instead of saying hello or waving or something civilized like that, he jerked his chin at me . . . just like Logan always did. It made my stomach tumble just a bit.

"And you, Cassidy?" Mr. Kouropoulos said.

Victoria nudged me and I jumped. "I'm sorry. What?"

"I trust you found your accommodations to be satisfactory?"

"Oh. Yes, thank you," I said quickly. "My room is really nice."

He nodded, smiling—obviously pleased with himself.

By then, Nikos had sauntered over to where we stood. He'd put on his Dolces, even though we were well under the shade of the awning, and jerked his chin at me again when I looked at him. Give me a break.

"Hi, Nikos," I said.

"Kalispera," he said. "That means 'good afternoon.'"

"Kalispera," I repeated.

"Kalispera," Zoe said softly beside me.

He didn't answer her, but I wasn't sure if it was because he was being rude or because he hadn't heard her. I couldn't see his eyes behind the sunglasses so I didn't know if he was even looking at her. I waited for a few really uncomfortable seconds until I couldn't stand it anymore.

"So, Zoe was just telling me this is her favorite spot on the yacht. What about you? Where—"

Zoe made a scared little squeaking sound and scurried away from us.

I watched her disappear into a hallway behind the elevator shaft. "What happened?" I asked. "Did I say something wrong?"

Nikos shook his head. "She doesn't talk much."

"She was talking just fine to me."

He shrugged.

"Shall we?" Mr. Kouropoulos said, bowing toward the table.

Four place settings. I looked to the crew, to Magus, to Victoria and Nikos and his dad, and then back to the table. So I was right about filming at lunch. Great. Even worse, the four of us would be eating in front of everyone else. My mom and dad were filmed during meals all the time, but with their show, I usually hung out with the crew so it wasn't often I had to try to eat gracefully with a camera in my face. But if they could do it, so could I.

I raised my chin and threw back my shoulders and said in my most genuine voice, "Yes, thank you. Everything looks great."

Nikos pulled out my chair for me while Mr. Kouropoulos did the same for Victoria. So genteel. I was actually proud of myself for being able to smile and ignore the cameras and settle into my chair somewhat gracefully. Mr. Kouropoulos started gushing about what a pleasure it was to have us on his yacht, and I thought I did a reasonable job of acting like I was interested, even though I was pretty sure he was about as sincere in what he was saying as I was listening to it.

In the background, I couldn't help but notice Zoe watching him, shaking her head just the slightest bit, a frown etching deeper and deeper on her face until it looked like she couldn't take it anymore, and she backed away. By then, she was standing directly behind where CJ stood with her clipboard, next to the cameras. I tried to catch Zoe's eye, but I caught CJ's instead.

Too late, I remembered I wasn't supposed to look at CJ when we were being "candid."

"Cut!" she yelled.

I don't know what the Greek word

for smorgasbord is, but that's what Zoe's mom had prepared for us. Nikos said the lunch was made up of *mezedes*, which he eloquently explained was "a bunch of hot and cold dishes."

To me, it looked like a lot of appetizers. I mean a *lot* of appetizers. They reminded me of the tapas you can get in Spain. I hoped that the rest of the crew would be eating, too, because there was way too much food for just the four of us.

Some of it I recognized, like olives, meatballs, octopus, and squid, but a lot more, Nikos had to explain to me. There were *kolokithea keftedes* (fried zucchini balls), *gavros marinatos* (marinated anchovies), *lakerda* (tuna in olive oil), *tzatziki* (a yogurt cucumber dip), some giant beans that I never did get the name of, and a whole lot more that I didn't get the chance to ask about.

While we were eating, we were supposed to be acting like we were having a stimulating conversation. But since I didn't know either Mr. Kouropoulos or his son, it was kind of hard once we moved past food and were supposed to find something else to talk about. And I was supposed to show enthusiasm! Be peppy! Smile! Laugh! (According to CJ.)

By the time the meal was over, I was totally drained, but I kept the smile going as long as the cameras were still rolling. And I wasn't the only one—as soon as CJ yelled cut for the final time, Mr. Kouropoulos pushed away from the table, and Nikos pulled out his cell phone to resume his texting. I sat there awkwardly wondering what I was supposed to do. Excuse myself from the table? (Whose permission was I supposed to get?) Stay put? Clear the dishes?

"Did you like it?" Nikos asked.

"What?"

He tucked his phone back into his pocket. "The food. Theia Alexa chose the menu especially for the television show. Your mom does the food on your show, right? What did you think?"

"It was good. Well, most of it," I admitted. I wasn't a big fan of squid. "Who's Theia Alexa?"

"She's the chef. She's not really anyone's aunt; she just likes us all to call her *theia*." Nikos pushed back in his chair and started to get up. "Come with me," he said. "I'll introduce—"

"Sit." CJ was standing behind Nikos and clamped a hand on his shoulder, pushing him back into his seat. "I need a couple of shots with just the two of you." She turned to Victoria. "Would you mind?"

"Not at all," Victoria said, and left the table.I wondered if CJ was going to film without sound, because Mr. Kouropoulos, was now pacing back and forth by the railing, practically yelling into his phone and waving his free hand around like he was trying to swat a bee or something.

Nikos, I noticed, was watching his dad, too. Sadly, I thought, but his dark eyes held something else. Anger, maybe.

Until CJ yelled to start. Then his face transformed. Suddenly, he was laughing, flirting, acting more like the guy who pulled me over to wave at the paparazzi. I tried to match his enthusiasm, and pretty soon I forgot I ever thought anything was wrong.

When they were finally done filming, and the crew started packing up, Nikos asked me if I wanted to go swimming. "There's a pool on the main deck," he said.

I was about to tell him I'd love to join him when Victoria shook her head. "Lessons first."

I turned in my chair so that my back was to Nikos and whispered to Victoria, "You're not serious."

"I'm completely serious," she whispered back.

"But we just got here!"

"It's past four, and we dock in Mykonos before eight. We'll be lucky to get in our three hours. You signed the agreement with your parents," she reminded me, "not to mention the network rules."

"But—"

"We should get started," she said aloud.

"I'm sorry, Miss Victoria," Mr. Kouropoulos said. "Could I speak with you first? It will only take a moment."

And then to Nikos, "Would you mind showing Cassidy to her room?"

Nikos was at my side in a second. "Come with me," he said, and he winked at me. Winked!

"I don't need anyone to—"

"It's fine," Victoria said to me. "Go ahead."

"Come on," Nikos said, and held out his hand.

Okay, so Victoria had made me read up on Greek culture the whole flight over, but I hadn't seen anything that would tell me what to do at that moment.

I wasn't sure if he wanted me to hold his hand or if he thought I needed help getting out of my chair or what. I was pretty sure I could stand without help, thank you, but again, I didn't know what the custom was, so I took his hand. His skin was warm and soft, and his grip was firm. So firm that I had to yank my hand away to get him to let go once I was standing.

He laughed at that. "Excellent," he said. "I can tell this is going to be an interesting week."

I followed Nikos down a wide set of stairs that led from the top deck (the sky deck, he called it) to the promenade deck. I was glad to see more of the yacht instead of just taking the elevator back down, although Nikos wasn't much of a guide. I mean, he knew where we were going, but he didn't say much along the way to tell me about what we were seeing. If it was me, I'd be pointing out every little detail. Zoe had showed way more pride in the yacht than he was. Maybe I'd ask her to show me around later.

"So," I said, "how did you learn to speak English so well? You hardly have an accent."

"I have cousins in Florida," he said. "Sometimes I go stay with them when my dad travels."

"Does he travel a lot?"

He shrugged. "I guess."

I knew what that was like. But then again, when my mom and dad traveled, I usually went with them.

We fell into silence again. I didn't like silence; it made me feel uncomfortable and awkward. So I kept trying to think of something to say to fill the empty space.

"What's your favorite spot on the yacht?" I asked finally.

He looked at me like I had just asked if he breathed water or air. "My favorite spot?"

"Sure. Zoe said her favorite is the sky deck because it has such an awesome view. Where do you like to hang out?"

He thought for a moment, and then his eyes lit up. "I'll show you," he said. He grabbed my hand, and this time I didn't worry about pulling back. It was kind of cool to be caught up in his enthusiasm. He led me down another flight of stairs and through a seating room that was all polished wood and white upholstery like the salon, only not as big. Finally, he showed me a narrow corridor.

"Hardly anyone comes down here," he said. "They're all too busy working or whatever."

"What is it?" I asked.

"You'll see."

Nikos stopped at the end of the corridor, in front of a wooden door with a brass plate that read, HERACLES. "Close your eyes," he said.

"Um, okay . . ."

I could hear the latch click as he opened the door. He pulled me forward. I slid one foot along the floor and then the other, squinting and trying to see where I was going through my eyelashes until he yanked on my hand and warned me, "No peeking."

Even through my closed eyes, I could tell that he had turned on the light. He moved me forward a couple more steps and then stopped. "Okay," he said. "You can open them now."

I had prepared myself to see another spectacular view. Or maybe a media room or something. So when I opened my eyes, I could only stand and stare.

"It's a game room," Nikos announced.

Which was an understatement. The room was filled with about every game you could think of: a pool table, a foosball table, one of those carnival basketball hoops, shelves full of board games. "Wow." I looked the room over. "It's huge."

"Runs about half the length of the yacht," he agreed.

Taking a few more steps inside, I turned in a slow circle. "This is amazing."

I expected one of his half-joking answers, but he just nodded. "I couldn't believe it when I found it down here."

"Found it?" I asked.

But he had already moved on, pointing out a wall lined with game consoles. "Look at this. They've got everything. Wii, Xbox, PS3 . . ."

"They?" I asked. "Who are—"

"Huh. Someone's been down here." He let go of my hand and walked over to where one of the screens showed a scene from some kind of medieval character game. "This is the game I play," he said almost to himself.

Since we didn't always have a game console or even a TV when we traveled for my mom and dad's show, I didn't get to play video games much, so I didn't know that much about them. I murmured something appreciative, because I figured that's what he wanted to hear. But Nikos wasn't listening to me anyway. He had walked over to the PS3 (I do know enough to tell the different systems apart) and picked up the controller. After he pressed a couple of buttons, a score flashed on the screen.

He whistled and shook his head. "Someone topped my high score."

"Didn't you say hardly anyone comes down here?" I asked.

But he wasn't listening; he was scrolling through what looked like a list of stats. "Whoever this player is, is good."

"Uh-huh," I agreed. Which wasn't very eloquent, I admit, but like I said, he wasn't listening to me, so I didn't figure it mattered. Once he connected to that game, it was like I wasn't there in the room with him anymore. I turned from him to look around on my own, when a movement caught my eye.

There. By the pool table . . .

I wasn't sure until I got a little closer, but then I could see her, crouched behind the rack of cues: Zoe. I quickly glanced back at the screen Nikos was studying so intently. Interesting. Was Zoe the mystery player? Made sense, although it didn't explain what she was doing, hiding in the dark. Maybe she didn't want Nikos to know she had played his game. Or . . . maybe she'd get in trouble for being there at all. Mr. Kouropoulos seemed like the type who wouldn't let "the help" play in his game room.

Zoe stared at me with round eyes, shaking her head just enough to signal that she didn't want me to tell Nikos she was there.

I nodded to let her know I understood, and turned back to where Nikos was scrolling through stats on the screen. "So," I said. "This is your favorite game, huh?" I stood directly behind him so that his view of the door would be blocked, and motioned for Zoe to make a break for it. "What's it about?" I asked.

Nikos looked at me like I'd just sprouted horns on my head. "Are you kidding?"

"Hey, I don't get to play these kind of games much."

He *tsked* and started pulling up different characters on the screen. "Okay," he said in a talking-to-an-idiot voice, "there are five character classes," he said, "elf, dark elf, knight, prince, or magician. Only the princes can lead a blood pledge."

"Is your character a prince?"

"Of course," he said smugly.

"What does it mean to 'lead a blood pledge'?"

He shook his head sadly and began to explain—slowly—the strategies behind the game. I admit to only half listening. I was more focused on the shuffling behind us. The soft click of the doorknob. The door closing as Zoe slipped out of the room.

I couldn't help but smile to myself. Zoe had been in here playing Nikos's favorite game. She must not have had time to turn it off when we came in. And, judging by the way Nikos had scrolled through the stats, she was good. Score one for Zoe.

By the time I got to her room,

Victoria was starting to get impatient. "Where have you been?" she asked.

"Nikos was just showing me around the yacht."

"All this time?" She showed me in, and I sat at her desk. "It's big," she said, "but not that big."

"Well, they've got a game room. . . ."

"Ah, that explains it."

"Nikos wanted to show it to me," I said. "I couldn't be rude and tell him no."

"Of course. You are nothing if not polite."

I didn't miss the sarcasm in her voice. "I'm sorry I kept you waiting," I said.

"Not to worry. It gave me a chance to speak with Magus. He lent us a book on Greek philosophy to add to your studies."

I groaned. "Philosophy?"

"Please," she said drily. "Curb your enthusiasm. I will read through it first. In the meantime, you"—she opened a book and set it in front of me—"may start by reading about the history of Delos."

I have to admit that I just sort of skimmed. It's not that I didn't find the stories interesting, it's just that I kept thinking about the game room. Zoe, hiding out in the dark. Nikos, so intrigued by the high score on his game. There had to be a story there, too.

"Have you finished your reading?" Victoria asked.

My thought bubble popped and I blinked, the page coming into focus again. How long had I been staring off into space? "Um . . ."

"I'd be happy to extend your studies if you are unable to complete your work in the allotted time."

"I read some of it," I protested.

"I see. Shall we review?" She pulled back her long, black hair and twisted it into a bun, skewering it with a pencil to hold it in place. Her business bun, I called it. Which meant she was settling in for the long haul. "Delos is the birth-place of . . . ?"

Ha. I knew that one. We were going to be talking about it during our shoot the next morning. "Artemis and Apollo."

"Well. I'm impressed." She turned a page in her notebook. "What does the word *delos* mean?"

I thought for a moment. Luckily, I knew that one, too. "*Delos* is visible. Before Artemis and Apollo were born there, Delos was supposed to be a floating island they called *Adelos*, which means invisible."

She glanced up at me, pleased. "Yes. Very good."

"It's in my lines for tomorrow," I admitted.

"I see. Do your lines say what significance its location had on Delos's prosperity?"

That one I didn't remember. "Does it have something to do with Poseidon?"

"Yes. In a way. Poseidon is said to have anchored Delos in the center of the Cyclades islands. It made Delos an important trade destination."

"Oh, right." It was coming back to me. "So a lot of people and business and wealth came to Delos, just like Apollo's mom said it would."

"That's right."

"So what happened? Why is it deserted now?"

Victoria closed her book. "As often happens, the wealth and prosperity on the island made it a tempting target for invaders. Rule of the island changed hands several times. People moved away. Eventually pirates and thieves claimed anyone and anything left behind, until one day"—she spread her empty hands—"gone."

I tried to imagine what it would be like if a busy, prosperous city like New York or Paris became deserted and just stopped *being*. "Could that ever happen now?" I asked. "A whole society dissolving like that?"

"Of course," Victoria said. "Think about the ghost towns from your Old West, or deserted steel towns once the industry moved out. The only constant in life is change."

"Is that something you read in Magus's book?" I asked.

"No. But there was a philosopher names Heraclitus . . ." She flipped through a few pages until she found what she was looking for. "He talked about how you could never step into the same river twice, because the water is always flowing, moving on."

"Meaning what?"

"Nothing stays the same. Fortunes change. What man *does* with that change is another discussion entirely."

I thought about that for a moment. Nothing was the same for me as it was just a few months ago. Now that the boy I liked was traveling with my mom and dad's show, I was not. My fortune had certainly changed. The question was, did I have the power to change it back?

Travel tip: The Greek people are renowned for their hospitality and generosity to foreigners.

We docked at Mykonos harbor just before sunset. Mr. Kouropoulos, Victoria informed me after our lesson, had invited us to join him and Nikos in the town for dinner. That's what he had wanted to talk to her about earlier.

"You'll want to dress nicely, but comfortably," she said. "He said we would be doing quite a bit of walking."

Which it why I was still standing in front of my closet when I felt the thrum of the engines change. I knew we were coming into port. I couldn't decide what I had that qualified as "nice, but comfortable." To me, comfortable was my favorite jean shorts with the hole in the pocket. They also fit my definition of *nice*, but I knew that wasn't what Victoria—or Mr. Kouropolous—had in mind.

I finally settled on the bold, blue tank dress I had grabbed in London before our Spain trip. I'd never gotten a chance to wear it because of everything that happened in Valencia, so it was still brand-new. Plus, it was the only designer thing I'd brought with me—which doesn't usually mean that much to me, but let's face it: We were going out to dinner with Greece's favorite leading man and his heartthrob son. We could pretty much count on an audience. With cameras. I did have my reputation as *la chica moda* to think about.

I had just pulled the dress on over my head when I felt the engines change again. Outside my balcony doors, I could see the busy port and the whitewashed buildings that seemed to rise up straight from the water.

I smoothed my dress down and rushed out onto the balcony to get a better view. The warm air smelled fishier than what I remembered of the harbor in Athens. In the turquoise water around us, single-masted fishing boats and huge yachts were tied to the piers, side by side. I leaned over the railing so I could see where we were docking, and my breath caught. I was right!

A crowd had already gathered at the end of the pier. I didn't see any barricades like before, but I did notice several men in dark suits standing in a row at the front of the crowd. Holding them back, most likely.

Someone knocked on my door, and I hurried inside to answer it.

"Are you ready?" Victoria asked. She looked even nicer than usual in a strapless, floral-print sundress, her hair swept back into a French twist. Her lips were shiny, I noticed. She was wearing lip gloss. She never wore lip gloss. I ran my tongue over my own un-glossed lips and wondered if I should put something on them before I left.

"I just need to get my shoes," I said, and ducked back into my room. I grabbed my silver strappy sandals from the closet, and a tube of lip balm from my bag by the desk. "Okay. Ready."

Nikos turned into a movie star again as we stood on the deck, waiting for the yacht to dock at the port in Chora, Mykonos Town. He didn't just wave to the crowd gathering on shore; he winked, pointed, posed, and mugged—just like his dad. I didn't know whether to be embarrassed or to join in.

That is, until we were finally anchored and it was time to disembark (a fancy word for get off the yacht). That's when I could hear some of the voices in the crowd calling my name. I mean, how could I not get into it after that? Besides, to my mom and dad, this trip was a test. What better way to prove to them that I belonged with their show than to play to my fan base? (How I had any fan base in Greece, I had no idea, but still.)

After everyone else had gone ashore, CJ and her crew filmed Nikos, his dad, Victoria, and me disembarking. It wasn't for any segment; it was just B-roll footage. B-roll is the background-type images you see between scenes that give a program its sense of place. Doing an arrival B-roll reminded me a lot of when Daniel filmed my mom and dad and me getting off the train in Buñol, Spain. Except Daniel had been using a single, on-the-shoulder camera instead of a complete setup with lighting like this crew.

And in Spain, Logan had been there, on the platform. . . .

"Cut!" CJ yelled. She clomped up the gangplank muttering to herself. "Cassidy, dear. As much as I enjoy your thoughtful expressions, we are going for carefree and happy right now. Do you think perhaps you could try to smile? Very nice. Okay." She spun around and marched back down to the pier. "Again!"

● ● ● ● ●

I was relieved when CJ and crew went off to film more B-roll without us in it. It wouldn't have been any fun walking around Mykonos being directed at every turn. I wished some of the crowd the cameras had attracted would have gone off with them, but we weren't so lucky.

It didn't seem to bother Mr. Kouropolous, though. He was very good at shutting out the cameras, and yet playing to them at the same time. The best I could manage was to remember to be *on*, but to try and forget they were there. I wasn't very good at the forgetting part.

It wasn't long before the sun was slipping steadily toward the horizon, casting long shadows and painting all the white buildings in a rosy light.

"The restaurant will be expecting us shortly," Mr. Kouropolous said, "but perhaps you would like to see the town first? It is really quite charming at sunset."

As we passed the cluster of paparazzi and curious onlookers, the dark-suited men I had noticed from my balcony fell into step alongside us. With Magus, they surrounded us in a tight formation. The crowd followed like an obnoxious, camera-flashing herd of sheep.

"This is crazy," I told Nikos. "When I go out with my mom and dad, there's sometimes a crowd, but nothing like this."

He shrugged. "You get used to it."

Mr. Kouropoulos must have overheard us because he

turned to me. "I apologize for the frenzy," he said, "but thought you ladies might like to walk among the shops before we dine. If it's too much for you—"

Shops? That was the magic word. "Oh, no," I said quickly. "It's no problem. And . . . I do like to shop." I gave him a smile, but inside I was kicking myself. The last thing I wanted to do was to offend our host. That wouldn't go over very well with the network. Or my mom and dad.

We left the busy harbor front and walked down a rambling, stone-paved street lined with colorful shop fronts and street displays.

"Is it true," Victoria asked, "that the narrow, winding streets in Mykonos were designed to confuse invading pirates?"

I'm pretty sure she was asking Magus, but Mr. Kouropolous piped in. "So I've been told," he said. "You'd best keep close." He took her hand and tucked it in the crook of his arm. "It is just as easy for beautiful ladies to become lost in the maze as it was for marauding pirates."

Victoria's smile went stiff, but she allowed him to guide her through the streets. I mean, what was she going to do?

"Smooth," I murmured.

"Not really," Nikos grumbled under his breath.

Most of the shops, I was disappointed to see, were the same kind of designer shops you find at any airport or tourist spot—Cartier, Hermès, Bulgari. "Aren't there any real Greek shops?" I asked.

"Not on this street," Nikos said. "Hold on." He tapped his dad and said something in Greek.

Mr. Kouropoulos turned and looked at me curiously. "You prefer to shop local, do you?"

"When I can," I said in a small voice.

"Do you know what you're looking for?"

I didn't. I mean, until I saw what there was, I didn't know what I wanted to buy, but that didn't sound like a very good answer. "Um, I'd like to find a charm for my necklace," I offered.

"I'm sure we can accommodate." He pulled his phone from his pocket and started speaking into it rapidly. Then he waited, cupping his hand over the microphone. "My assistant is finding directions."

He signaled to Magus and pantomimed writing something onto his hand. Magus quickly pulled a pen and a small notebook from his pocket and handed them over. Mr. Kouropoulos scribbled down some words on a sheet of paper and ripped it out of the notebook.

"We are quite close to a local artist's shop," he told me when he hung up. "Come this way."

Off the tourist path, the streets became even narrower. They were still paved in the same flat, gray stones, but the buildings themselves were less uniform. Bright doors and window shutters cheered up the long sea of white. Steep stairs climbed up and out of sight at odd places. Balconies jutted overhead. "I love it," I breathed.

I reached for my phone to take a picture of the street and then realized I had left it sitting on the desk back in my cabin after I had uploaded the pictures for my blog. I nudged Nikos. "Would you mind taking some pictures for me? I forgot my camera."

"Sure." He didn't even hesitate, but pulled out his phone and pointed the camera at me. "Smile!"

I threw up my hand to block the lens. "No, not me! The street. For my blog."

"Ah, yes. The famous blog. Then you should be *in* the street," he declared, and pointed the phone camera at me again. "Better yet, we should be in the street together!"

Before I could move, he grabbed me by the shoulders and pulled me close, holding his phone at arm's length to take the picture. Again, I was reminded of Buñol, when Mateo, Logan, and I were watching the fireworks. We had lain back in the grass, our heads close together, and I held my camera out to take pictures, just like Nikos was doing now. If I imagined it clearly enough, I could almost feel Logan's head against mine.

I reached up absently and smoothed back the hair where our heads would have been touching. Just then, flashbulbs popped somewhere nearby, startling me from my walk down memory lane. I realized Nikos wasn't the only one taking pictures.

"That's good," I said, pulling away from him. "Thanks."

"Anytime," Nikos said with a wink.

I shook my head at him. For someone who didn't seem to like his dad's come-on moves, Nikos sure had them down himself.

"Ah, here we are." Mr. Kouropoulos ushered us toward a small storefront with a gleaming display of jewelry in the window. Most of it was gold. And fancy.

I swallowed hard. The kind of jewelry this store sold probably cost a fortune. I usually just bought my charms from street vendors. But after Mr. Kouropoulos had diverted the walk and looked up a jewelry shop just for me, how was I going to gracefully get out of there with my allowance still safely tucked away? Especially when he was holding the door open for Victoria and me to enter. What could I do? I walked inside.

I have to admit, the jewelry was much more interesting than the mass-produced stuff on the designer-shop street. Delicate, artistic, unique. I found myself drawn to the display cases, even though I knew I could never afford anything in them.

In one of the cases lay a collection of pendants that featured round blue stones with dots in the middle of them. "They look like eyes," I said.

"They are." Nikos stood next to me, looking over the display. "Those are the evil eye. They're supposed to protect you from harm."

I ran my fingers over the Italian *cornicello* charm my grampa had given me. That was supposed to give me good luck, which I supposed was close to the same thing. When I got back to the yacht, I'd have to tell him about it on my blog.

"Did you see one you like?" Mr. Kouropoulos asked.

They were all pretty much the same, just in different settings. And they all seemed to be staring at me. But then I noticed a small one made with a dark lapis stone. Because of the texture in the stone, the circle in the center was subtler than the others. And with the gold filigree setting, it looked more like an art piece than an eye. "That one's nice," I said.

"Very well." Mr. Kouropoulos snapped his fingers, and the shopkeeper hurried to open the case for him. I cringed as they pulled the velvet-lined display board from the case and unpinned the charm for me to look at closer. How much would it cost? It was only our first night. If I bought it, would I have any money left for the rest of the trip?

"Let us see how it looks on that necklace of yours," Mr. Kouropoulos said, handing it to me.

I turned it over, trying to slyly get a peek at the price. It wasn't marked. "I'd have to tie it on," I said.

"Go ahead," Mr. Kouropoulos prodded.

Slowly, gingerly, I undid my necklace and laid it on the

counter, and slipped the evil eye onto the leather cord so that it dangled with the other charms. I had to admit it looked completely awesome. "How much is it?"

Mr. Kouropoulos waved his hand like he was trying to clear smoke from the air. "It is no matter. If you like it, you shall have it."

"But I don't know if I can—"

"Nonsense. You are our guest. I will get it for you."

I hesitated. What was I supposed to do? In some cultures, I knew it was rude to turn down a gift. Was this one of them? I looked to Victoria for input, but she was looking at some other pieces in a different case. Nikos wasn't much help, either. He was busy typing something into his phone. "Well . . ." I began.

Mr. Kouropoulos wasn't even listening to me. He was already at the register, paying for the charm.

"Here," Nikos offered, taking my necklace from the counter. "I'll hook it for you."

He lifted the cord over my head, and I turned my back to him, holding up my hair so he could fasten the clasp. "Thanks," I told him.

"You're very welcome," Mr. Kouropoulos answered benevolently.

I wanted to make sure Nikos knew the thanks has been directed to him, too, but he had already taken a step back and let his dad take over. I was starting to get the feeling he did that a lot.

The restaurant Mr. Kouropoulos took

us to was built right into the side of a hill. I'm serious. It looked like the building grew straight out of the rock. The maître d' welcomed us at the door and escorted us through the main dining area. It was crowded with round tables draped in white tablecloths, and patrons who stared and whispered behind their menus. Someone in the back got bold and snapped a picture, the flash punctuating the electricity in the air.

"Is this what it's like every time you go out?" I whispered to Nikos.

"When he wants it to be," he said.

I was about to ask him what he meant by that when the

maître d' stopped to open a narrow door to a private room set with a single table and four cushy chairs. Magus and one of the other bodyguards stood at attention on either side of the door while the man ushered the rest of us inside.

"I've taken the liberty of ordering," Mr. Kouropoulos said as we settled around the table. "The chef here is known for his traditional approach to Greek cuisine. Your mother would appreciate his methods, I think, Cassidy. Perhaps you can entice your parents to bring their show here in the future."

"I'm sure they'd like that," I said. As if my mom or dad would ever take location tips from me.

A line of waiters began bringing in food. I guess since Mr. Kouropoulos had ordered beforehand, it was ready and waiting for us. I could get used to that kind of service.

The smell of roasted meat and spices filled the room, and my stomach rumbled. I thought I'd never be hungry again after the lunch we had that afternoon, but my appetite returned the moment I saw the food.

"Are those stuffed grape leaves?" I asked Nikos.

"*Dolmathes,* yes," he said. "And this is *spanakopita.*" He pointed to some phyllo-dough triangle things, and then to some skewers threaded with cubes of meat and vegetables. "And that is *souvlaki.*"

The rest of the meal looked a lot like the dishes we'd had at lunch—salad, olives, some kind of stewed vegetable.

"And for you," Mr. Kouropoulos said to Victoria, "*Ouzo*." He poured a thick, clear liquid into two small glasses and handed one to her.

"What is that?" I whispered to Nikos.

"Traditional drink. We can't have it because it's liquor."

"Oh." I watched Victoria closely. In all the time I'd known her, I'd never seen her drink anything stronger than green tea.

She lifted the glass to her lips and took a tiny sip. "Oh, very nice," she said. "It really does taste like licorice."

And that was it. The glass sat untouched the rest of the meal. She was always so good at handling stuff like that. Straightforward. Polite, but sure of herself. The way I wished I could be.

It didn't take long to realize that Mr. Kouropoulos had ordered way too much food. Dishes kept coming and coming until the waiters had to take some of the plates away half eaten to make room for more.

I tried to sample at least a taste of everything, because that's what my mom and dad had taught me to do. It didn't matter what culture you were in; if someone went to the trouble and expense of preparing a special meal for you, it was only polite to show your appreciation by enjoying it. Or at least pretending to.

I was glad the Greek culture wasn't one of those that said it was insulting not to eat every scrap of food. Because by the time they had brought out the baklava for dessert, all I could think about was getting back to the yacht for my upcoming talk with Logan. If we'd have had to hang around and stuff the rest of the food down our throats, I think I would have screamed.

As it was, I practically ran to the pier. Or I would have if we weren't surrounded by bodyguards who didn't feel the same urgency I did to get back to the yacht. I don't even remember if I said good night to Nikos once we got there.

Victoria took her time strolling down the hallway to our rooms. I wanted to leave her behind and bolt for my room, but then I'd have to explain why I was in such a hurry and I kind of preferred keeping the video chats just between Logan and me. Not that there was anything wrong with us meeting online or that our parents wouldn't approve or anything like that. Just . . . liking a guy can be awkward enough. Liking a guy when everyone in your life knows about it is impossible.

"I would like to have spent more time on Mykonos," Victoria said. "It's such a lovely island."

"Lovely," I agreed. *Hurry!*

"So much more to explore than what we saw this evening."

"Yeah. A lot more." *Hurry, hurry, hurry!*

"Perhaps *When in Rome* could come here. It's been years since they've done Greece."

"I don't even remember it," I said.

I swear, Victoria was being slow on purpose. Getting

through the conversation was like trying to run through waist-deep water. No matter how fast I tried to wade through the words, we weren't getting anywhere.

Finally, she stopped outside our doors. "Here we are," she said cheerily.

"'Kay. Good night."

"Good night," she said.

And then, as I was unlocking my cabin door, she added, "We have an early start time in the morning, so don't stay up long."

I looked sharply at her. Did she know about the chat? "Go to bed. Got it." I turned to the lock once more.

"Cassidy, you know you can come stay in my room if you get lonely, yes?"

I was glad my back was to her so she wouldn't see the relief on my face. That's what the stalling was all about? Sweet, but did she think I was five or something? I always slept in my own room when we traveled, and I never got lonely, thank you very much. Of course, my mom and dad were always sleeping in the room right next to mine. . . .

"Yeah. Thanks," I said through a weirdly tight throat.

"Right." Her tone was brisk all of a sudden. "Good night, then."

My door was halfway open, but I stopped and turned back. "Victoria?"

She looked up from the key in her hand. "Hmm?"

I gave her a quick hug. "G'night."

"Good night, Cassidy," she called after me as I rushed through the door and closed it behind me.

I was late. Only by minutes, but still, what if Logan didn't know I got his message? What if he signed on and saw I was dark and thought I couldn't make it?

Kicking off my sandals on the way, I ran to the desk and dropped into the chair, quickly booting up my computer. The time clock appeared on the screen and I winced. I was five minutes late. It doesn't sound like a long time, but believe me, it can seem like hours when you're waiting for someone. How long would Logan wait?

I signed into the chat window. No Logan. Fair enough. He might have checked in and then gone off to do something else like I had done that afternoon. I sat back in my chair and waited. And waited. And waited. Logan's icon stayed dark.

He did say ten my time, didn't he? I checked his note in the message box. Yup. Ten o'clock. I waited some more. Still no Logan. Maybe he didn't wake up; it was six in the morning his time. Or maybe Cavin was up and wouldn't let him get on the computer. Or maybe he really did mean ten in the morning my time.

Disappointment began to settle on me in layers, each one growing heavier and heavier until I had to push away from the desk to shake it off.

I moved the cursor over to the sign-out button, and my

finger hovered over the mouse for a second, but I couldn't make myself click on it. I'd been looking forward to this chat all day, and I didn't want to admit it wasn't going to happen. Still, wishing wasn't going to make him magically appear. Logan's status still showed he was offline. If he wasn't there, he wasn't there.

It was the hesitation that saved the evening for me. Because right before I pushed the button that would have logged me out, the computer made a phone-ringing sound, and Logan's icon lit up. All my disappointment and insecurity evaporated. I clicked on the call message to start the chat.

"Hey! There you are," he said.

A wave of hot-and-cold tingles washed over me, the way they did whenever I saw his face on my screen. "Hi!" I waved at him and he waved back. His movements looked a little choppy from the connection, but I could see him and hear him and that was all that mattered.

"How is it, then?" he asked.

"Amazing! You wouldn't believe how beautiful it is here. What about you guys? How is New Guinea?"

He shrugged. "Not bad."

"That sounds really positive."

"No, really. It's not bad. Where we are, there's not much to do, but at least it's . . . pleasant. Not like when we did that one show in Greenland."

"Hey, that would have been really pretty in the summer."

"Too bad we were there in the winter."

"Hello. I think winter was your dad's idea."

"Well, he was daft. So you like it on the boat?"

I laughed. "It's a yacht."

His image on the screen did a choppy eye roll. "Same thing. It's big. It floats. What about your costar? How is he? You like him?"

I hid a smile. Logan's words had become clipped as he asked about Nikos. Was he jealous? "He's all right," I answered. "We haven't really done much yet. Only the B-roll shots."

"So you'll be spending a lot of time with him this trip."

"I suppose." I said the words casually, but inside I was laughing. This was perfect. Logan *was* jealous! He wouldn't be jealous if he didn't like me as more than a friend, right?

"What will you do all day?" he asked.

"Oh, you know, the usual. Cruise around the islands. Lounge in the sun. Oh, and we went into Mykonos tonight and had dinner. And I got a charm for my necklace, see?" I held up the evil eye charm in front of the webcam.

"Very nice. Did he go with you?"

There it was again. The jealous tone. I hid a smile. And sidestepped the question by changing the subject. Because being jealous was one thing, but I didn't want it to spoil the conversation.

"You should see the game room they have on this thing!"

I told him. "One whole wall is just a bunch of TV screens with about six game consoles and a whole library of video games. It's crazy."

Logan perked right up, just like I thought he would. "What do they have?"

I told him about Nikos's favorite, and we spent the rest of the call talking about games—which ones rocked, which ones sucked, and why. Like I said before, I didn't really know that much about video games, but Logan had become quite the connoisseur while he was in Ireland with his mom. I let him carry the conversation. Mostly because I liked to listen to him talk. Too soon it was time to end the chat.

"I hafta get offline before Da gets up," Logan said.

"Can you log on tomorrow?"

"Sure."

"Same time?" I asked.

"Yer killin' me," he said with an exaggerated yawn, "but I'll try."

He signed off, and his icon went dark again. I sat still, staring at it, imagining what it would be like to talk to Logan in person again. We could go for walks together. Maybe hold hands. And then, when the setting was just right—like on a Tahiti beach under the moonlight, or in Paris at Christmas when the Champs-Élysée is lit by a million sparkling lights—Logan might even kiss me.

At least I could dream, right?

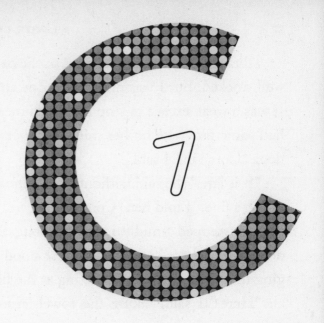

A knock on the cabin door startled

me out of my daydream. I closed the computer and rushed over to answer it.

Zoe stood in the hall, holding—more like hugging—an armload of towels. She let her eyes meet mine for only half a breath, and then she stared at the floor.

"Well, hi!" I said. When she didn't answer, I asked, "You want to come in?"

She threw a nervous glance up and down the hallway before answering in a whisper. "I . . . check to see if you have plenty, um . . ."

"Towels?" I asked helpfully.

"Yes. Towels," she agreed.

I'd taken only the one shower, so the bathroom was still well stocked. But I was pretty sure Zoe already knew that. It was a weak excuse to stop by, which meant she probably had something else on her mind. I stepped away from the door. "Come in," I said.

"It is late," she said without conviction.

"It's fine," I told her. "Come on."

She stepped timidly into my cabin, and I closed the door behind her. And then she just stood there, still hugging those silly towels, still staring at the floor.

"Here," I said, taking the towels from her. "I'll take these. Have a seat."

Without waiting for an answer, I hurried off to put the towels away in the bathroom. When I came back, Zoe hadn't moved.

"Is everything all right?" I asked.

Finally, she looked up at me, and I was surprised to see the concern in her eyes. "You don't tell?"

"Tell what?"

"It was me," Zoe said. "I played the game."

Oh. That's all? I was kind of disappointed.

"You . . . don't tell"—Zoe's voice dropped—"him?"

"Him? You mean Nikos?" I asked.

She nodded and looked to the ground again.

"I didn't say anything," I said. "But even I did, why would he care?"

"I did not ask to play. It is his game."

I didn't get it. Why was she so worked up? Nikos didn't seem like the kind of guy who would get mad just because someone played his game. In fact, he wasn't upset when he was showing me the scores Zoe must have earned; he was impressed. "He said you were a good player," I said. "I mean, he didn't know it was you, but he showed me how you outscored him."

"I know!" Zoe wailed. Which was not great for the whole stealth thing she was going for. I figured at that point we should probably bring our powwow deeper inside the cabin instead of right next to the doorway.

I took her hand. "Come on. Let's sit down."

She hesitated for a minute, pulling back against my grip. "Oh, no. I—"

"Please, Zoe," I said. "I could really use the company."

"You?" She cocked her head to one side and her face changed. Relaxed. The scared-rabbit look faded from her eyes and was replaced with concern. "You are . . . okay?"

"Yeah, I'm—" I was going to say I was fine, but the eagerness in her posture changed my mind. "I just need someone to talk to. Are you busy?"

She smiled that beautiful smile of hers. "No. I can . . . talk."

We sat on the white couch facing each other. To be honest, I didn't have any idea what we would talk about. It just seemed like a good thing to say at the moment. If I'd had any practice at girl talk, it might not have been so hard, but I didn't really get the chance to hang out with girls my age that much. Okay—ever. Which was the point, come to think of it, of my mom and dad sending me to live in Ohio. They wanted me to have a "normal" life like a "normal" teenager. Only I didn't want normal. I wanted to stay with *When in Rome*. And Logan.

Although I will admit I liked the idea of having a friend to talk to—even if I didn't know what to say.

"I'm nervous," I admitted to Zoe. "About the shoot tomorrow. I've never done a whole segment with speaking parts before."

She nodded seriously. "I understand."

That's all it took. I spilled my whole need-to-impress-the-parents story. It's not what I had planned at all, but Zoe listened, nodding, murmuring encouragement at the right places, and I couldn't stop once I got going.

"How about you?" I asked. "How long have you worked on the yacht? Have you known Nikos's family for a long time?"

"Oh. No." She looked over her shoulder as if she wasn't sure we were alone and leaned closer, lowering her voice. "I am not—"

But before she could divulge what she was not, someone knocked on the door. She jumped to her feet, and her eyes darted around the room. Almost as if she was looking for a good place to hide.

"Cassidy?" Victoria called through the closed door.

"Is everything okay?" I whispered to Zoe.

She shook her head frantically. "I should not be here . . . bothering the guest . . . after the bedtime. . . ."

"Cass? Are you awake?" Victoria called softly.

I steered Zoe toward the bathroom. "Quick. In here. I'll get rid of her."

She dipped her head and slipped inside just as I opened the hall door.

"Weren't you in bed?" Victoria asked.

I realized I was still in the dress I'd worn into town. "Um. Not yet. I was on the computer." Which was the truth, earlier. "I'm supposed to post updates on my blog every night." Also true. I didn't have to tell her I had already uploaded the photos that afternoon.

"I see." She glanced beyond me into the cabin. To where my computer lay closed on the desk. "I'm sorry it's so late, but CJ asked me to give you tomorrow's updated itinerary." She rattled a sheet of paper in her hand.

"Updated? But we just got it."

Victoria nodded. "Yes, but apparently there have been some changes. We need to be ready to go ashore at seven. Do you need me to wake you?"

"Nah. I have an alarm."

"All right, then." She handed me the paper and took one last glance around my cabin. "Lights out as soon as you get ready for bed."

"Got it," I assured her, and closed the door. Then I watched through the peephole to see Victoria close the door to her own cabin.

"It's okay. She's gone."

Zoe came out of the bathroom, all flustered again. "I must go," she said.

I sighed, disappointed. Anything Zoe had been about to tell me before Victoria interrupted was locked up tight again.

"Okay. Hold on," I told her, "I'll check to see if the coast is clear." I opened the door and checked out in the hallway, looking both ways before I gave her the go-ahead.

Zoe thanked me and started to dart out of the room, but I stopped her. "Anytime you want to talk," I said, "my door is always open."

She at me, startled. *"Parakalo,"* she said. "Thank you." And then she was gone.

In the fugitive bathroom, I brushed my teeth and washed my face and wondered what Zoe's secret was. Besides hiding out in the game room, I mean. And as I drifted into a twilight sleep, I replayed the events of the evening. This assignment wouldn't be boring, that was for sure.

Patience is bitter, but its fruit is sweet.
—Aristotle

Our 7:00 a.m. sound check came

extra early because I had to show up to hair and makeup by 6:30. Nikos was lucky he was a guy and he didn't have to sit in the chair for so long. Especially since the makeup artist—Jacqueline, she told me with a sniff—acted like she'd gotten up on the wrong side of the bed that morning.

"What is this thing?" she asked, lifting the leather cord of my charm necklace with one manicured finger.

I grabbed the necklace protectively. "It's my good-luck necklace," I told her. "I got it from my grampa."

"How touching. I'm going to need you to take it off."

I tightened my grip. "Why?"

"Darling, work with me here."

"What's wrong with it?"

"Is there a problem?" CJ walked past and peered at me over her clipboard (did she ever put that thing down?).

I settled my necklace on top of my shirt. "Not as far as I'm concerned," I said.

"Well, let's hurry it up then, shall we?"

Jacqueline's lips pursed, puckering like she'd pulled a drawstring to close them, but she didn't say anything more about the necklace. Still, if I thought I had won, I was dead wrong. She made sure I knew she wasn't happy with me, tugging my hair as she brushed it, pulling it tight as she wound it onto heated rollers. I never thought I'd say this, but I missed Daniel and the soft touch he had when he did my makeup and hair in Spain.

I glanced at the watch on Jacqueline's wrist as she clipped in the last roller. "Are we going to have time to finish this?" I asked. "It's already six forty-seven."

"Oh, we aren't going to brush it out now," she said. "It would just get blown around on the boat. We'll wait until just before the shoot."

"But . . ." I ran my fingers over the mass of rollers in my hair.

She slapped my hand away and yanked a scarf around my head, tying it securely on top. "This will keep them in place."

"You mean I have to go out to the island like this?"

"Of course." She started packing up her kit. "What did you think?"

I bit my tongue so I wouldn't tell her what I thought. That would only make her dislike me even more. My chest felt hollow and heavy at the same time. I missed Daniel all over again. He would never have tried to make me feel small.

A sudden wave of homesickness for my mom and dad and the *When in Rome* crew made my throat ache and my eyes sting. I blinked quickly to keep tears from forming. Yes, I was tired and overemotional, but it was only the second day away on my adventure. No way was I going to start acting like a baby. All crying would do was ruin my makeup. And make Jacqueline angry that she had to do it again.

The smell of fresh bread caught my attention, and I swiveled in my chair to see Zoe and her mom and a lady in an apron and head scarf setting up a breakfast table on the deck. My stomach grumbled, and I checked the time. I still had ten minutes before we were supposed to begin. That should be enough time to grab something to eat.

The offerings on the table were simple: some kind of white cheese, sliced tomatoes, olives, bread, dark tea, and honey. The culture book I had read explained that a traditional Greek breakfast is based on something a shepherd could pack up and take out to the field with him. Greeks didn't usually eat a lot in the morning. Instead, they had a pastry and some fruit or something as a midmorning snack, and ate a large lunch late in the afternoon.

Simple looked great to me, though, and my mouth watered as I waited behind a couple of the crew members for my turn at the plates.

Zoe looked up from the platter of sliced bread she was carrying and gave me a hesitant smile, like she wasn't sure how to act around me after last night. I waved and said, "Calamari, Zoe!"

She hid her smile behind her hand, and her shoulders began to shake as she tried to hold in her laughter.

"What?" I asked.

"You say to me 'squid,'" she said, giggling. "For 'good morning' it is *kalimera*."

"Oh!" I laughed with her. If she only knew—squid was nothing. I'd made much worse language mistakes. *"Kalimera,"* I repeated.

Suddenly, Zoe's laughter stopped. She dropped her eyes to the table and started messing around with the plates and napkins, straightening them into perfectly parallel rows.

Nikos and his dad were just arriving on the deck, gesturing and posing like they were making an entrance onto a stage. I glanced back to Zoe to make a comment about how silly Nikos looked, when I noticed she was watching him, too—with kind of a happy-sick look on her face.

Oh.

Oh!

Zoe had a crush on Nikos! Is that what she was going tell me before Victoria knocked on the door?

I thought about how upset she had been that she had played his video game without permission—especially when she beat his top score—and it all started to make sense. No wonder she acted so straight-faced and timid whenever he was around.

"Hey," I said under my breath, "are you—"

But Zoe took off—for the safety of the kitchen, I supposed. I watched her retreat, and a new goal formed in my head. We had nine days left of the cruise. Nine days to get Zoe and Nikos together.

I took my breakfast back to the makeup chair and ate as carefully as I could so I wouldn't spoil the color Jacqueline had painted onto my lips. The cheese, I decided, was a little sour for my taste, but I liked the bread and the tomatoes.

I had just finished eating when Nikos dropped into the chair next to mine, yawning. *"Kalimera,"* he said.

"Kalimera," I answered.

He rubbed his eyes and looked at me a second time. "Nice look for you."

For half a second, I wondered what he was talking about, and then I remembered. "Why, thank you," I said, patting the scarf-wrapped curlers on my head. "Are you ready for this?"

His gaze slid over to where his dad stood talking to Victoria and CJ. I couldn't read the look on his face. But then he smiled and shrugged. "Too late to back out now."

I hated to admit it, but Jacqueline was right; my hair would have been blown all over the place on the speedboat ride to the island. As we raced across the water, the wind whipped the ends of my scarf and snaked down my sweater, making me shiver. If I didn't have my hair rolled up, it would have been a mess by the time we reached the island.

Victoria had chosen to ride over earlier with the crew to set up the equipment, so it was just Nikos and me riding with Magus this trip. Mr. Kouropoulos was nowhere to be seen. At first I wondered why he wasn't coming with us, but when it came right down to it, I didn't really care. Nikos looked happier and more relaxed than he did when his dad was around.

I watched him as the boat skipped over the water, laughing into the wind, his dark curls blowing back from his face, and I was actually glad his dad wasn't there to spoil it.

About halfway to Delos he turned to me and yelled over the speedboat's motor. "Let's go up front! We'll have the best view!"

I shook my head. "Too much wind. I'm cold!" I hugged my arms and shivered in illustration, but he was unimpressed.

"Suit yourself," he said, and climbed up to stand alongside Magus.

By then, I could see the island up ahead, a completely different world from what we had just left in Mykonos. From the boat, we could already see some of the ruins. It was eerie, knowing that so many people had once called the island home. They had lived among those ruins. They probably thought the island as it was would go on forever. I thought about what Heraclitus wrote. You can never step in the exact same river twice. *Fortunes change.*

But Victoria said it was what a person does with their situation that counts. Maybe part of that meant enjoying the moment—because if all things change, it couldn't go on forever. I pulled my sweater tighter and crawled up to join Nikos and Magus in the front of the boat.

We began filming the first segment in front of Apollo's temple. The crew had cordoned off an area with nylon rope and already a handful of curious tourists had begun to gather. Jacqueline finally took out my hair curlers and touched up our faces as the sound guys ran one last check. Then it was time for us to deliver our tremendously corny lines. Seriously. Whoever wrote the script probably thought it sounded a whole lot cleverer than it actually did. Meanwhile, not only did Nikos and I have to say the silly words, we had to look really excited about it in the process.

I just kept reminding myself that it was all for a good purpose. If I delivered the lines for the network, maybe they'd deliver me to *When in Rome*. Seemed like a fair trade-off.

● ● ● ● ●

"*Kalos irthate stin Ellada!*" Nikos beamed at the camera. "Welcome to my country, Greece! I'm Nikos."

"And I'm Cassidy."

And then in unison, "We want to show you the magic light of Greece."

I scratched my head. "Nikos, what is the magic light of Greece anyway? Is it really magic?"

"Well, Cassidy," he replied, "you tell me. Look around."

I scanned the marble ruins around us.

"What do you think?" he asked.

I winked at the camera. "Magic!"

"Cut!" CJ yelled. "Cassidy, what was that?"

My hands went cold. What did I do wrong? I know the lines were stupid, but that wasn't my fault. I wasn't the one who thought of them.

"You sound as if you're half asleep," she said.

I also wasn't the one who changed the shoot time to seven thirty in the morning.

"Now let's take it from the top. Nikos, your line. Ready, and . . . action."

"*Kalos orisate stin Ellada!*" Nikos said. If at all possible, he sounded even perkier than the take before. "Welcome to my home—Greece! I'm Nikos."

"And I'm Cassidy!"

"Cut!"

● ● ● ● ●

We ran through the same awful introduction about a dozen times. CJ kept yelling at me, even though I swear I wasn't doing anything wrong. I wanted to cry, but it wouldn't have done any good. She'd probably just yell some more.

I missed the way we did things with *When in Rome*. Our cameramen never yelled at anyone because they weren't delivering their lines the way he wanted them to. And they also didn't want anyone acting like an animated Barbie, either.

Nikos commiserated with me between takes. "Maybe we should act like we're talking to three-year-olds," he said. "Make it more bouncy and bubbly."

"Are you kidding? If I was any more bubbly, I'd float away."

But he was right. I put a whole lot more bounce into my lines, and she stopped yelling quite so much.

The only way I made it through that morning was by hamming it up with Nikos. We made a game out of seeing who could be the cheesiest—which wasn't hard with the kinds of lines we'd been given.

The funny thing was, the cheesier we got, the more CJ liked what we were doing. By the end of shooting, we could have created an entire moon of cheese.

"I can't take ten whole days of this," I told him when we were done. "It's making my teeth ache."

"It could be worse," he said.

"How?"

"You could have been stuck with a cohost who was not

as devastatingly good looking as me." He struck a he-man pose.

"You gotta stop reading about yourself on the fan sites," I said. "You'll get a big head. Oh, wait. Too late for that."

"I'll start worrying when there isn't anything about me in the fan sites to read." He laughed, but I had a feeling he was at least partially serious.

I was about to make a smart remark about that when Victoria walked up to us with her notebook in hand. "We should get started," she said. "We have to head back to Mykonos at one."

"What are we doing?" Nikos asked.

"*You* don't have to do anything," I told him, "but *I* have to put in my three hours of schooltime. We're going to take a tour of the ruins as part of my homework."

"Sounds like fun," he said. "Can I come?"

"Really? Did you hear the part about it being homework?"

He clutched one hand over his chest. "It is my history," he said dramatically. "Of course I am serious."

I giggled. "Well, if you're going to put it that way . . . okay."

Can I just tell you right now that there is no way to see everything on Delos in just an hour and a half? We'd shot in only two sites—the Hermes shrine at the Agora of the Competialists, which was, like, this huge, open marketplace close to the harbor, and then in front of the pillars of the Temple of Apollo (of course)—so we had a whole island left to see when we were done with the segment.

The crew had gone around to take B-roll footage before we got there (ironically, although we were talking about the magic light of Greece, they wanted to get their shots done before it became too bright). So they packed up and started ferrying back to the yacht while we took in as much as we could.

"Hurry," Victoria urged as we hiked over the stones. "There is so much I want to show you."

The whole island was like a museum. Everywhere we looked, broken pieces of buildings and pillars lay on the rocky ground like bleached bones of long-dead animals. Wind whistled past the columns that still stood. Scattered remnants of statues rested in the dusty weeds.

We practically had to run to keep up with Victoria, she was so anxious to show us everything she could.

"We'll start on the north side of the island with the Terrace of the Lions," she said, "then work our way back to the harbor."

There wasn't much terrace left in the Terrace of the Lions, just what looked like an overgrown field surrounded by a crumbling stone wall and a line of huge, eroding marble lions atop rough stone pedestals. The whole area was roped off so we couldn't get very close, but it was probably the kind of place best admired from afar so you could see the whole thing anyway.

"How big do you think those lions are?" I asked Nikos.

"Big enough to eat you."

"Ha-ha. Very clever."

"Look at how the weather has worn down the marble," I said.

"Not really," Nikos said. "These are fake. They put the real statues into the museum to preserve them."

I nudged Nikos. "Well, look at you, brainiac."

He gave me a strange look. "Brainiac?"

"Smarty-pants," I clarified.

"What are you talking about?"

"Know-it-all."

"Oh." He grinned. "Yes, I am all knowing."

"Then you know Victoria is leaving us." I pointed to where Victoria was walking down the path. We had to run to catch up with her.

"Look at the architecture of these houses," she said.

I didn't know how she could tell they had been houses. Broken pillars and fallen walls were all that was left of them.

"Look," Nikos said dramatically. "The architecture of a commode." He pointed out what looked like a stubby column that swelled to a circle on the top. The circle had a hole in the middle.

I laughed. "You would notice that!"

"It is a valid observation, Cassidy," Victoria said. She went on and on about the water-and-waste-management system the island had in place—fascinating for the time period, she said. Maybe. But seriously? The island's sewage was the last thing I wanted to spend my morning talking about.

"Good going," I told Nikos under my breath.

He shrugged. "I do what I can."

At one point, Victoria informed us we were looking at the House of the Tritons. I imagined a bunch of trident-wielding mermen hanging out in there—you know, like King Triton from *The Little Mermaid*? But I was wrong.

"Look at this floor!" I called. "Is that a woman Triton?" I had only ever seen a guy Triton before. I didn't know it was an equal-opportunity position. But there she was, with a long, curling tail, and a winged, naked baby flying above her head.

I pulled out my phone to take a picture of her while Nikos and Victoria climbed over the fallen stones and pillars to where I stood.

"Oh, yes," Victoria said. "She is called a Tritoness."

"What's with the cupid?" In my mind, Tritons and cupids didn't quite go together.

Nikos laughed. "That is Eros," he said. "Cupid is Roman."

"Whatever. He looks out of place with her."

He shrugged. "Maybe the Tritoness needed a little help with her love life."

"Actually," Victoria said, "Eros had a strong connection with the sea. His mother was Aphrodite, who rose from the sea."

"It's amazing that the floor is in such good shape," I said. "How could those thousands of tiny pieces of tile survive for all these years when the big marble building around it didn't?"

"Well," Victoria said, "size is not always the determining factor for strength. You can't judge the worth of a thing—or a person—based on how it looks. Things are often not as they appear."

"I'm sorry," I said to Nikos. "She can't help herself. She has to turn everything into a teaching moment. It's a disease, really."

Victoria chuckled. "You know you love it."

As we hiked down the hill, our feet hit the gravel in a kind of crunching rhythm. Victoria's words echoed in my head. You can never tell the worth of a thing by how it looks . . . how it looks . . . how it looks. Fortunes can change . . . can change . . . can change. It's what a man does that matters . . . matters . . . matters.

Was it possible, I wondered, to make your own fortune?

C9

We hadn't even seen a quarter of the island before we realized it was time to head back to the harbor. Strike that. It was *past* time to head back to the harbor. We speed-walked back, kicking up the dust behind us.

"Quickly," Victoria said, her breath coming in short puffs. "Magus will be waiting."

I had to double-time it to keep up with Nikos's long strides. Until then, the sun hadn't seemed hot, only pleasant and warm. But now it was beginning to feel like a blowtorch on my skin. The fabric under my arms and along my waistband had become uncomfortably damp. I wanted to ask if we could slow down for a little bit, but I didn't want Nikos to think I couldn't keep up.

By the time we reached the harbor, I was out of breath and glistening. (Daniel once told me that girls don't sweat; they glisten.) And Magus wasn't there.

"Maybe . . ." I said, panting, "we're late."

"Maybe he's late," Nikos said. (Not even breathing hard. How is that possible?)

"Hold on." Victoria pulled out her phone. "We'll soon find out." She spoke to someone on the other end for a minute and then tucked her phone back into her bag. "As I thought," she said. "He had to run some of the crew back to the yacht, and he's coming back to get us."

"Then we can see more of the island?" Nikos asked.

She shook her head. "He's already on his way. We should stay nearby."

I was glistening in full force by then. "I'm going to test out that water while we wait," I said. The pier we were standing on was just yards away from the rocky beach, and all that lovely, cool (I hoped) water was calling my name.

"I'll come with you," Nikos offered.

"You two go ahead," Victoria said. "I'll let you know when I see Magus coming."

At the edge of the water, I kicked off my sandals and stepped gingerly on the gravelly shore. Bits of rock and shell poked at the bottoms of my feet, but not enough to stop me from wading in. I sighed with relief as the cool water closed over my feet and lapped at my legs.

"I can't believe how clear the water is!" I said.

"Of course. What do you think water is supposed to be like?" Nikos asked.

"If you go to some oceans," I said, wading in farther, "you can't see anything beneath the surface. Not clearly anyway. We went to the Pacific Ocean in California once, and it was, like, grayish green. Not clear blue like this."

"The water isn't blue," Nikos said, wading in next to me. "It's clear, as you said. The color is a reflection of the sky."

I squinted up at him. "Wait. Is that true?"

"Partly," he said. "At least that's what my tutor said."

Ha! So he did have a tutor. "You said 'partly.' What about the other part?"

"You want the scientific answer?"

I shrugged. "If that's the one you've got."

He cleared his throat and stood straighter. "White sunlight," he said authoritatively, "contains all the colors of the spectrum. Water molecules absorb the light, but they absorb the red light more than the blue light, so that blue light is what you see. And since it takes a lot of water to get the effect, different depths show up as different shades of blue."

"For real?" I asked.

"It's science."

"See? I told you you were a brainiac."

"Why do you keep saying that?"

"If you're so smart," I said, "you'll figure it out."

"Whatever you say." He turned away slowly. Then, before I could react, he bent down and splashed a handful of red-absorbing water at me.

I squealed and splashed a handful back at him. Before long, we had a full-on water fight going. I was thoroughly soaked (and loving it) by the time I heard Victoria's voice above the sound of the splashing.

"Wait." I held down his arm so he couldn't splash anymore. "Did you hear that? What did she say?" I shaded my eyes and looked to the pier, where Victoria was waving us over.

"Time to go," Nikos said. "Magus must be here."

We sloshed back to the shore. I had to step slowly and carefully over the sharp bits.

"Can you move any faster?" Nikos asked.

"It's these rocks," I said. "My feet are sensitive from being in the water for so long."

"Put on your sandals," he said with a "duh!" tone to his voice.

"My sandals are leather. I don't want them to get wet."

"Are you serious?"

I nodded.

"Who wears sandals they don't want to get wet to a beach?"

"I didn't know we were going to be going to a beach."

Victoria yelled for us again, and Nikos grumbled. He turned his back to me, kind of stooping over like he was suddenly an old man.

"Get on," he said.

"What?"

"Get on my back," he said slowly, like he was talking to a child. "I'll carry you."

"Oh. No. You don't have to—"

"They're waiting."

I looked back to the pier, where Victoria stood with her hands on her hips. "What if I'm too heavy for you?"

He just laughed. "Grab your sandals," he said.

It's been years since I'd had a piggyback ride. In fact, the last time I could remember was when I was about five and my grampa used to carry me around their farm. It might be little-kid-ish to say, but having Nikos carrying me was kind of fun. I would have preferred it to be Logan, but I could always pretend.

He set me down on the pier and, since my feet were dry by then, I slipped my sandals back on. Nikos climbed into the boat first, and then turned to help Victoria and me.

I took his hand and climbed down as gracefully as I could, considering that the waves lapping at the sides made the boat bob up and down. I wobbled over to one of the cushioned seats and sat down while Nikos helped Victoria onto the boat.

He came over to sit by me, resting his arm along back of the cushions behind me. I sat uncomfortably straight-backed so his arm wouldn't accidentally "slip" and end up around my shoulders. I hoped he hadn't gotten the wrong idea when we were splashing in the water. Or when I let him carry me back to the pier. Or help me into the boat.

I know, it's crazy. Nikos was the cutest guy I'd ever met, besides Logan, of course. And maybe Mateo in Spain. He was definitely crush-worthy, but I was hopelessly stuck on Logan. Besides, Zoe liked Nikos. So as cute and fun as I thought he was, I just didn't like Nikos that way.

I scooted to the edge of the cushion just enough that I could turn and talk to him without being obvious. He didn't seem to even notice, much less care.

"Someday," I said, "I need to come here again and see everything we missed."

He shrugged and tried to act bored. "I have been there many times. After a while, all the ruins look alike."

"Are you kidding?" I laughed. "Hello. I was there with you. I saw how you reacted. You thought it was amazing, too. Admit it."

"It was interesting."

"It was more than interesting. That place was *ancient*. Don't you know how cool that is? Your history goes back forever. My country's history goes back only about two hundred years."

"The history of America as a *nation* may be two and a quarter centuries old," Victoria corrected, "but the history of the land and its peoples dates back much further than that."

"Yeah, well, we don't have any ruins like these," I said.

"What about the Anasazi cliff dwellings? Or the Serpent Mound in your own Ohio?" Victoria *tsked*. "I can see we need to add some American history lessons to your studies."

"See what I mean?" I said to Nikos. "Everything is about studying!"

I think Victoria was about to say something else, but just then the motor roared to life and the boat slid away from the pier. We flew toward the yacht, bumping over the waves. I was happy to ignore Victoria and her teaching moments for a while. All I wanted was to feel of the wind rushing through my hair and the sea spray on my face.

Nikos leaned closer and yelled, "Look!" He pointed to a boat maybe a football field's distance away from us, racing through the water parallel to ours.

"Who is it?" I yelled back.

"Paparazzi. They found us!" My breath caught for a second, but Nikos seemed delighted to see them. Almost like he had been expecting them. "Wave!"

I shaded my eyes to get a better look. The boat was a smaller version of the one we were in. One man stood at the wheel, steering, while another balanced on the seats, snapping pictures with a bulky-looking camera.

"Telephoto lens," Nikos shouted. "Better check your teeth before you give him a smile."

I quickly ran my tongue over my teeth. It was a habit, ever since I got my stupid palate expander . . . which I wasn't wearing because I had forgotten to put it back in. Good for the camera, not so good for me. I'd pay for it later.

Nikos laughed at me. "You are perfect. Now, smile!"

He was really hamming it up, gazing off into the distance, flexing his muscles. He looked back at me and winked, grinning. Like I said before, his grin was contagious. It wasn't long before I was playing to the camera alongside him, pulling out my best movie-star poses and making pouty faces and generally having a good time. Until Magus decided to outrun them and the boat jumped forward. I tumbled back onto the seat, practically landing on Victoria's lap.

"Strange that they should show up now," she said.

"Why?" I asked. "They know we're docked in Mykonos. They're probably just following us around."

She glanced back to where the paparazzi boat was growing smaller and smaller behind us. "I wonder," she said.

Travel tip: It is considered very

bad manners in Greece to make noise during the afternoon nap time.

By the time we got back to the yacht, CJ and the camera crew had already slipped off to go over the day's footage. The yacht crew was scurrying around, preparing to cast off. From the savory smell that hung in the air, Theia Alexa was busy making lunch. With all the bustle on board, and after the early makeup call, our walk around Delos, and the post-adrenaline crash from our paparazzi chase across the water, I was beginning to feel deliciously drowsy.

Victoria must have been feeling it, too, because she

yawned and announced that she was going to go lie down for a bit and rest before lunch.

"Ooh. That sounds like a good idea," I said.

Nikos looked at me like I was crazy. "You're kidding, right?"

"What? It's not acceptable around here to take a little rest?"

"Not unless you're an old *yia yia*," Nikos said. "Besides, *mesimeriano ipnako* is not until after lunch."

"Am I supposed to understand a thing you just said?"

"A *yia yia* is a grandmother," he told me in a mock-patient tone. "*Mesimeriano ipnako* is a siesta. Only old women would take a nap so early in the day."

I crossed my arms. "I didn't say I was going to take a nap."

"What are you going to do when you lie down, then?" he asked. "Count ceiling tiles?"

"Maybe if there were ceiling tiles in my room," I said haughtily. "Which there are not."

"Oh. Huh."

"What? Do you have ceiling tiles in your room?"

He hunched his shoulders. "Not tiles, exactly, but you know what I mean. There's that kind of a pattern in the wood inlays that looks like tile."

"Oh, nice," I said. "You have a wood-inlay ceiling?"

"Yeah. Don't you?"

"Um, no." I bumped his arm. "Don't you know what the rooms look like in your own yacht?"

"Oh, uh, yes," he said. "Of course I do. I just forgot which cabin you were staying in."

"Well," I said, holding back a yawn, "if it's socially unacceptable to rest before lunch, what is there to do on . . ."

My words trailed off as I noticed Mr. Kouropoulos strolling onto the deck. He spotted us and sauntered over to where Nikos and I stood. "Ah. Back from the ancient city, I see. Did you have a good time?"

I realized he was talking to me and nodded, trying to re-engage my power of speech. "Oh. Yes. It was . . . I really . . ."

But then it didn't matter, because the way his eyes strayed immediately, I knew he wasn't even listening. "Nikos," he said, "may I have a word?"

I excused myself quickly and hurried away. Not to my cabin, though, because strangely enough, I wasn't tired anymore.

I wandered over to the railing near the back of the *Pandora* and pulled my phone out to film the yacht pushing away from the pier. The deck under my feet rumbled as the engines engaged and we put out to sea. Behind me, Mr. Kouropoulos raised his voice. I couldn't help glancing back at them. I wasn't trying to be nosy; it was more like a reflex. I couldn't hear what Mr. Kouropoulos was saying, but whatever it was, Nikos didn't look too happy about it.

Nikos glanced up, and I looked away quickly. Suddenly, I felt like an intruder. I left the railing and found the steps leading to the upper decks. The smell of Theia Alexa's cooking was stronger a floor up. I followed my nose to the kitchen, hoping I could find Zoe there.

I found her rolling out thin sheets of dough on a marble-topped table, humming to whatever she was listening to on her iPod.

"Hey, Zoe," I called to her. She didn't hear me. Duh. The music. I walked closer and leaned down, ear level, to try again. "Hi, Zoe. What are you making?"

She jumped and the rolling pin slipped from her hands, rattling across the table before it clattered onto the floor.

"Cassidy." She pulled the earbuds from her ears. "You scare me."

"I'm sorry." I picked up the rolling pin and handed it to her like a peace offering.

She dropped it into a sink of sudsy water and grabbed another one from a wide, shallow drawer underneath the tabletop. "You film at Delos this morning, yes? You . . . have fun?"

It was a simple question, but the way she asked it— almost wistful and maybe a little sad—made me hesitate a beat before answering. Besides Nikos and me, Zoe was the only other kid I'd seen on the yacht. *What must it be like,* I wondered, *to be the one who has to work while the other two play?* Well, okay, technically we were working, too, but only for four hours a day.

"I don't know about fun," I said. "It took me about ten takes to get the segment right."

"And Nikos?" She concentrated on rolling the dough and only glanced up at me from beneath her dark lashes like she was embarrassed I might see her blush at his name.

"It's okay, Zoe. I think he's really cute, too."

She stopped rolling the dough. "You do?" she asked weakly.

"Sure." I pulled up a tall stool and sat next to her. "And I'd probably be crushing on him right now if it wasn't for Logan."

That did it. She glanced up quickly, hopefully. Zoe's face was like a book. With color illustrations. Anything she thought or felt was scrawled all over it for anyone to read. We'd have to do something about that.

She didn't ask, but I gave her an explanation anyway. "Logan travels with my mom and dad's show," I told her. "He's my best friend. Or . . . he was anyway. It's a long story. I think I probably like him more than he likes me, but I'm working on it."

"How will you . . . work on it?" Zoe asked.

That was a good question. I'd brought it up, but now I didn't know if I could define it for her. "Show him I'm interested, I guess. But not so it's obvious."

She nodded, but I could see on her face that she was confused. I wished I had a better explanation to give her. I wished I had a better explanation to give myself. I mean, I *hoped* Logan knew I liked him as more than a friend. And I hoped he liked me back. It sounded like maybe he did, the way he asked about Nikos. But I wasn't experienced with guys. Since we traveled so much, I hardly got to know any, so I didn't know what I was doing. For all I knew, Logan thought of me as just a friend. A buddy. A pal. Or worse, a sister.

I had no business trying to play matchmaker for Zoe when I didn't even know how to match myself. But that didn't mean I wasn't going to try. "How long have you liked Nikos?" I asked.

Zoe's expression now turned to panic.

"Don't worry," I assured her. "I won't tell him about that, either."

She relaxed a little and it looked like she was about to say something, but just then, Theia Alexa backed into the kitchen, carrying a huge, steaming pot. Zoe jumped up to hold open the door.

"Oh!" Theia Alexa said when she saw me, "Miss Cassidy." She set down the pot on the table. *"Kalispera."*

"Kalispera," I repeated. "Wait. I thought it was *kalimera.*"

"Kalimera mean good morning," Zoe explained. *"Kalispera* is good afternoon."

Theia Alexa set the pot down on the table and lifted the lid. The savory smell of meat and onions filled the air.

"Mmmm . . ." I sniffed the air. "What are you making?"

"Kreatopita," Theia Alexa said. "Meat pie."

"Smells awesome," I said. "Can I help?"

"We are almost done," she said, "but you can help Zoe set the table."

Travel tip: The Greek are very social. In Greece, it is very unlikely that one dines alone.

It was kind of depressing, setting the long table on the sky deck with only four plates. That table was meant to hold at least twelve people.

"Or more," Zoe said. "It has also extra leafs."

"Does he ever have a full dinner party here?" I asked.

She looked at me blankly. "Who?"

"Mr. Kouropoulos. It seems like he would have a lot of friends to invite onto the yacht for dinner. Have you seen any other famous people?"

She thought for a moment. "Yes, but not here."

I started to ask her what she meant when Theia Alexa called out from the kitchen. "Zoe!" She pressed her lips together. "I must go," she said, and left me alone with the dishes.

Lunch was probably delicious. I don't know; I was too keyed up to eat. Letting Nikos know that Zoe liked him was the best thing, I was sure. So why wasn't I so confident about following my own advice when it came to Logan? He was my best friend. But that could have been the problem. He was my best friend, and I didn't want to mess that up.

"Are you feeling well?" Victoria asked. "You've hardly touched your plate."

"I'm fine." I shook off the twinges of crew homesickness and stabbed my fork into a chunk of eggplant. "I was just thinking about something else."

"Well, be sure your thinking doesn't preclude eating. Theia Alexa would be distressed if she thought you didn't like her moussaka."

Sure enough, Zoe's mom was hovering near the head of the table, watching us eat (or not eat, in my case) with a disapproving frown on her face.

I took a bite to satisfy her. "It's very good," I said. Which was true. I took another bite. "I've had moussaka before, but this is . . . different. I can't tell what it is. The sauce, maybe? There's some kind of spice I don't recognize."

"I know what it is," Nikos said. He turned to Theia Alexa and said something in Greek I didn't understand.

Theia Alexa smiled and nodded. She answered him in Greek as well.

Nikos leaned back in his chair, obviously proud of himself.

"What?" I asked, completely lost. "What are you talking about?"

"I knew I would get it," he said.

"Get what?"

"My mother," Zoe explained in her soft voice, "say she

maybe should not admit it, because this recipe, it is a family secret, but . . . Nikos guessed correct."

His name from Zoe's lips sounded like a caress. And she blushed prettily when she said it, as if speaking his name out loud was some kind of special thrill. I stole a quick glance at Nikos to see if he could detect that as well as the mystery ingredients, but he was too busy congratulating himself on his tasting skills to notice. Guys are so clueless.

"So what is it?" I asked. "What's the ingredient?"

This time Nikos spoke up. "We can't tell you," he said. "It's a secret. . . ."

Zoe's smile grew wider, if that's even possible, and her cheeks took on a deeper shade of pink. You could almost see the thought dancing, skipping, turning somersaults in her head; she and Nikos shared a secret!

But then Nikos added, ". . . between Theia Alexa and me."

Zoe's smile faded, but Nikos kept grinning like an idiot. See? I told you—clueless.

After lunch, Victoria reminded me yet again that we were scheduled to resume lessons at four. Seriously, it's not like I was going to forget it in the twenty minutes since she reminded me last. I sighed dramatically and informed her that yes, I remembered that we were going to keep going since we hadn't put in a full three hours on Delos.

"We still have half an hour before we need to start," I said. "I'm going to walk around a little bit before then." It killed me to think of being cooped up inside when the sun was shining so cheerfully outside, and the water was so blue. Stupid agreement.

Victoria regarded me for a moment and then agreed. "Fine. I'll see you at four."

I watched her disappear into the elevator and slumped back in my chair.

"What is it my American cousin says?" Nikos grinned. "Oh, yes. Sucks to be you."

"What about you?" I asked him. "Don't you have to study?"

"I'm on holiday," he said. "No school."

"What about you, Zoe?" I asked.

She had been gathering dishes, and she looked up, startled. "What?"

"Are you on holiday? From school, I mean."

"Oh. Yes." She slid a quick—and longing—look at Nikos. "Holiday."

"Must be nice," I said with a sigh. I wished I could take a break from lessons, too, but—as Victoria constantly reminded me—I needed to study every day if I was going to keep up with my schoolwork. Because if I didn't keep up with my schoolwork, I wouldn't pass the proficiency exams, and if I didn't pass the exams, my mom and dad would think they were right when they decided I needed a more "structured environment" and that I should go back to regular school.

I pushed back from the table. "Well, if I have to go be stuck inside for a couple of hours, I want to walk around and get some sun first. You guys want to come?"

Zoe's face registered surprise, and then panic, and then something that looked like regret before she finally murmured, "I must do my jobs." She actually appeared to shrink as she folded over the plates she was gathering.

I was about to suggest that Nikos and I could help her finish, but Nikos was already on his feet, pushing his chair back in to the table.

"I'll come with you," he said.

Zoe turned away with her armload of dishes. I didn't know how to get her to come with us without being obvious. I'd have to find out more about her work schedule if there was going to be any hope of arranging for her and Nikos to spend time together.

I followed Nikos down the steps to the promenade deck—which was the one deck that wrapped all the way around the yacht without being broken up by stairs or something.

Nikos and I promenaded around the deck, lost in our own thoughts for a minute, and then Nikos said, "Tomorrow, since we don't have filming until evening, Magus promised to take us out on the boat."

I gave him a sideways look. "Um, we *are* on a boat."

"No. I mean on the speedboat. You know, like we took to Delos today. Have you ever been wakeboarding?"

I had to admit I hadn't.

"I'll show you how," Nikos offered. "If you don't have to study . . ."

"I'm only required to do schoolwork three hours a day," I said quickly. "I'm sure I can find the time to come out on the boat with you guys."

"It's a date then."

Date? He was probably joking—he was hardly serious about anything else—but I didn't want to even go there. Especially since the plan was to set him up with Zoe. I was trying to think of a way to inject her into the conversation when Nikos grabbed my arm and yanked me closer to him.

I pulled back. "Uh, hey, Nikos, I'm not—"

"Look," he said, pointing. "There they are again. The paparazzi."

Three white boats glided through the water behind us, looking more like toy boats from the distance. If they were paparazzi, I couldn't imagine they'd be able to get any good shots from that far away. Even with a really good telephoto lens, what could they hope to—

"Wait." I shook my head. "Those look like fishing boats. See the lines?"

He shaded his eyes and squinted at them. "Oh." His

shoulders drooped a little. Was it possible he was disappointed?

"Don't worry," I teased. "I'm sure they'll be back."

He looked at me strangely for a second and then shrugged. "Too bad you have your lessons," he said. "You'll miss your photo ops when they do."

"Ha. I think I'll live."

By then, we'd made almost a complete lap around the deck. As we came around the corner, I could see Zoe up ahead near the bow of the yacht, leaning against the railing, staring out over the water. She didn't turn toward us as we got closer, but I knew she was aware of us there, the way her posture stiffened and she stood unnaturally still.

Nikos, as usual, was oblivious. He kept chattering as if she wasn't even there. "Here," he said, pulling out his phone. "We should take our own pictures. I could post them on my Facebook page. Make all the other girls jealous."

Zoe kept staring at the waves like she didn't hear him, but I noticed the way she flinched when he said that.

"I've got a better idea." I broke away from Nikos and ran up beside Zoe. "Take *our* picture for your page."

Finally, Zoe turned from the water to look at me with wide, panicked eyes.

Grampa told me once how when wild animals are startled, their instinct is either to freeze where they are or to take off as fast as they can. I could almost see the same debate race through Zoe's head. I slipped my arm through hers to hang on to her in case she decided to try to escape and turned her so that we were both facing Nikos.

"Yes! Two girls! Even better for my image." He practically skipped over to where we stood, and pressed his cheek up against mine, holding the phone out at arm's length to take the picture.

"Wait," I said. "Shouldn't you be in the middle?"

"Good idea," he agreed.

Next to me, Zoe started to pull back so I tightened my grip on her arm until Nikos wedged himself between Zoe and me. When I was sure she wouldn't run away, I let go.

Nikos held the phone in front of us again. "Smile!"

Little by little, Zoe let herself relax until I'm pretty sure she was having fun posing with Nikos for his pictures. And when he paused to show us the shots on his screen, I know she was smiling for real. Laughing, even. If I was the jealous type, I probably would have been green with envy by then, because Zoe's smile was downright beautiful.

Nikos must have noticed that, too, because when he looked up from his phone and saw her laughing next to him, something changed. For an instant, the cocky, macho-guy mask fell away. He looked surprised and suddenly unsure.

And then her eyes met his and the same look of hesitation mirrored on her face. Both of them quickly looked away, but the attraction had been unmistakable.

It made me happy and sad at the same time. I suddenly really missed Logan. Had he ever looked at me like that? Would he ever look at me like that? Not unless I got my mom and dad to take me back with the show. Otherwise, I'd probably never be near him again.

I stepped back. "I have to go," I said. "My lessons."

Zoe and Nikos jumped apart, both rushing to answer.

"I should go practice," he started.

"I should help my mother," she said.

They exchanged another look—shyly this time, and then rushed off in different directions. I watched them go, and then trudged off to do my lessons.

Poor Victoria. I don't remember a thing she tried to teach me that afternoon. All I could think about was *the look*. For one small moment, Nikos had let go of his Don Juan act. That one moment was enough for me to catch a glimpse of who he really was—just a guy who wanted to be *liked*. If only he knew how crazy Zoe was about him. He didn't have to worry about that.

What I didn't get was if he really was a regular, nice guy underneath, why did he feel the need to act so full of himself all the time? Sure, he was a movie star's son, and sure, sometimes—even when he was putting on an act—he could be funny. Even charming. Imagine what he could be like if he wasn't trying so hard.

No wonder Zoe was crushing on him so bad.

I drew little nonsense doodles on my paper, wondering how I could let Nikos know Zoe liked him without scaring Zoe off in the process. I mean, to anyone with half a brain, it should have been obvious, but I'm convinced that sometimes boy's brains are not completely functional.

"Cassidy?" Victoria said.

I blinked back to the present. "Oh. Yeah. Sorry." I tried to find my place in the workbook, but it was hard to concentrate on that when all I could think about was the onboard drama.

It was clear what I had to do. I had to play Cupid. Or Eros, as the case may be. All it would take was a little push to get Nikos and Zoe together.

"Cassidy!"

I blinked at Victoria again. "Huh?"

She sighed and closed the mythology textbook. "Let's take a break for a moment, shall we?"

"I'm sorry. It's just hard to concentrate when—"

"I understand," she said. "You're on a beautiful yacht. You'd rather be off with your new friends. But learning is important, as well."

"I know. It's just . . ." I sighed. How could I explain it to her without telling her about Nikos and Zoe?

"Just one moment." Victoria grabbed a small book from her bedside drawer and held it out to me. "Magus lent this to me. He thought we might be able to use it for your studies."

I turned it over in my hands. It had a plain blue cover with a red spine, but no words. "What is it?"

"It's a book of quotations from some of the most famous Greek philosophers. I'd like you to choose three different quotes and write an essay for each, telling me what you think it means, and how it applies in your life."

"I have to write essays?"

"Or we could always do more math." She reached for the book.

"No," I said quickly. "I can read the quotes."

Have you ever had to do homework when you're on vacation? If so, welcome to my world. I'm on a yacht in the middle of the Greek islands, and instead of swimming or playing or lying around in the sun, I have to do three hours of homework *every day*.

Today I'm supposed to choose three quotes from famous Greek philosophers and write three different essays, explaining those quotes and how they could be applied in my life. Here are some quotes from Plato I think would be fitting. What do you think?

> *"Knowledge which is acquired under compulsion
>   obtains no hold on the mind."*

> *"I have hardly ever known a mathematician who was
>   capable of reasoning."*

> *"I'm trying to think. Don't confuse me with facts."*

• • • • •

Logan's icon was already lit when I signed on for our video chat that night. The familiar thrill tumbled over me, just seeing his picture. Was this what Zoe felt like when she looked at Nikos? At least she got to see him in person. How long would it be before I saw Logan face-to-face again? For now I'd have to be happy just talking with him. At least that was better than nothing.

"Good," he said when the chat went live, "I thought you weren't going to make it."

"What?" I glanced at the time clock in the upper corner of my screen, confused. "I'm not late, am I?"

"Nah. But I can't stay on long. Da will be up any time now. We're sailing out to Kimbe this morning for some cultural festival. The local ladies are going to show your mum the proper way to roast a pig."

I felt a little pang at that. I'd done the pig thing with my mom once. It was in Tonga, and we wrapped the pig in banana leaves and buried it in a pit lined with hot rocks. I wondered if they did things differently in New Guinea. It felt weird to know I wasn't going to be there to see it with her firsthand.

"So they're making New Guinea pig," I joked weakly. Anything to lighten my mood.

He just gave me a blank look.

"You know, like guinea pig? Those little furry— Never mind. Sounds like loads of fun."

Logan just laughed. "Hey, if there's food, I'm happy. And if I'm really lucky, there might even be fireworks afterward. Although I'd have to watch them alone."

My face flushed at the mention of fireworks. Did Logan remember that night in Spain the way I did? Back then, I didn't realize how much I liked Logan. And since then, I hadn't exactly told him. . . .

I thought about Zoe and her secret crush on Nikos—how I planned to make sure he knew, how I was going to get them together. Why was it so much easier to manage someone else's crush than it was to manage my own?

"Can you hear me all right?" Logan asked.

"Yeah. I'm sorry. I . . . was thinking about something else."

"Oh."

"But I was listening to you!" I hurried to add.

"It's okay. I hafta go anyway."

"Oh." My stomach sank right down to my knees. "Will you be around tomorrow?"

"I dunno."

Now my stomach hit the floor. Was it my imagination, or did he not sound very enthusiastic about it? "Same time?" I asked in a small voice.

"Yeah. Prob'ly."

"Okay. Well . . ." I forced a smile and tried to make my voice sound perkier than I felt. "Hopefully, I'll talk to you then."

He said good night and signed off. I turned off the computer and sat at the desk.

All alone.

Suddenly, I didn't like having my own cabin so much anymore. Maybe just for the one night, I could take Victoria up on her offer to stay with her. She'd probably think I was a baby, but I didn't care, as long as it meant I didn't have to be alone. Or to think about how the chat with Logan had ended and what it might mean.

Across the hall, I knocked softly on Victoria's door. She didn't answer. I knocked again, even though by then I was getting the empty vibe from her cabin. I closed one eye and squinted at the peephole in her door with the other. It looked dark inside. I knew it was past lights-out, but I kind of doubted Victoria kept the same hours she set for me. She was probably at another boring meeting with CJ or something. Which meant she wouldn't know if I wasn't in my room . . .

I know it was against the rules, but I couldn't face my empty room just then. Maybe I could find that game room Nikos had showed me the day before. It couldn't be too hard; the yacht wasn't *that* big.

If I just retraced my steps up to the deck where we had been talking the day before, and tried to follow our path down the stairs and through the huge sitting room and . . . yes. I found the narrow corridor.

By then I could tell that somewhere on the boat, someone was playing some Greek music. I didn't know that much about Greek music, except that it had a really distinct sound—and I'd heard it in movies before. This music was up-tempo, folksy with almost a rock beat. I was tempted to give up my search for a game and go find the music instead. It didn't sound like it could be very far away.

As it turned out, I didn't need to choose one or the other. The farther down the corridor I walked, the clearer the music became. I stopped outside the game room door. It sounded like the music was coming from in there.

Quietly, carefully, I eased the door open, expecting to see a party going on. Or some of the crew hanging out in there or something. But the game room was empty. Or almost empty. As I stepped inside, I saw Nikos sitting in the corner, holding something that looked like a mandolin, but with a really long neck. He was jamming along with the music playing on the stereo.

From what I could tell, he was really good. I couldn't even move my fingers as fast as his were dancing over the frets.

He was so into the music that he didn't even notice me come into the room. Which was just fine; I didn't want him to stop playing. I tiptoed behind one of the arcade games so I could listen to him out of sight. That's when I saw Zoe. She was sitting on the floor behind one of the other big games, eyes closed, her head nodding in rhythm to Nikos's music.

For half a second, I wondered if Nikos knew Zoe was there. No, that was stupid. Otherwise, she wouldn't be hiding. So . . . she was here listening to him in secret. I wondered if this was something she did often—like when I saw her hiding near the pool table the night before. Did she come here hoping to see Nikos? That would explain why she had been playing the video game in the dark. Maybe this concert was a nightly ritual with Nikos. The more I got to know him, the more I realized I didn't know Nikos at all.

I don't know if she could feel me there or if she heard me sit down or what, but all of a sudden Zoe's eyes flew open and she looked right at me with that same panicked fear I had seen in her eyes as that afternoon. She started to get up, but I shook my head quickly and held my finger to my lips. I hoped that was a universal sign for quiet.

She must have understood, because she settled back down again, even though she still had that cornered-animal look on her face. What did she think I was going to do? I mean, come on. I had helped her escape the game room *and* hid her in my room the night before. Didn't she know she could trust me?

Maybe not. We were still getting to know each other. Besides, my guess was it wasn't me she was worried about. She was probably afraid that Nikos would know she'd been hiding out, listening to him. I knew how I'd feel if Logan found me sitting there in the dark. I would be mortified. And here I had come in and blown Zoe's cover.

I eyed the door, wondering what the chances would be of sneaking back out the way I had come in. Nikos was still too distracted by the music even to know I was there. I motioned to Zoe to let her know I was clearing out, but I don't think she understood what I was trying to say. She shook her head frantically, *no*.

It's okay, I signaled to her as I stepped out from behind the arcade game. *I'm just going to . . .*

Uh-oh.

The music ended and Nikos looked up. Right at me. Maybe that's what Zoe was trying to tell me. She must have known the song was about to end. It was all I could do not to look back over to where she was crouched, but I didn't want to give her away. So I clapped for Nikos.

"That was really great. I had no idea you could play like that."

He pulled the instrument closer to him, like he was trying to protect it . . . or hide behind it. "How did you know I was here?"

I took a few steps closer to him—away from Zoe. "I didn't. I just followed the music to see where it was coming from and—"

The oh-crud-I'm-caught look on his face came a close

second to Zoe's. He switched off the stereo. "I thought the room was soundproofed. Could you hear the music all over?"

"No. Not really." I took another tentative step forward. "What kind of instrument is that?"

He looked down at the thing in his hands as if he was surprised to find it there. "It's called a *bouzouki*."

"I love the sound. So traditional."

He shrugged. "Sometimes."

"So . . . sometimes not traditional?"

He hesitated, like he was keeping some big secret and deciding whether or not he could tell. Finally, he looked back up at me. "Listen," he said. He changed the CD in the stereo and pressed Play.

I expected more of the Greek music I was familiar with, so I was surprised by the heavy bass beat. I didn't recognize the song, even though it did sound vaguely familiar. "This is rock," I said. Like he didn't already know that.

If Nikos heard me, he didn't show it. He bent over the bouzouki again and started . . . well, I don't know if "shredding" is the right word to use for a bouzouki, but the way Nikos played could put any guitar hero to shame.

When the song ended, he leaned back and closed his eyes, almost as if he had to gather his thoughts back together before he could speak again.

"Wow." I was so blown away, that's all I could come up with. "That was awesome!"

He looked up almost shyly and hunched his shoulders a little bit. "Thanks."

"Does CJ know you can play like that?" I asked. "We should do a segment on—"

"No," he said quickly.

"Why not? That was the coolest thing ever. Think of how much the network would love to promote—"

"That's just it," he said bitterly. "I don't want to be promoted."

"Oh." I didn't know what else to say. From the tone of his voice, I knew I'd hit a sore spot. "I'm sorry."

He took a deep breath and let it out slowly. "It's just . . . this is just something I do for me, you know? I don't want my dad to think it's just another thing he can use to get attention."

"Your dad?" The realization hit me slowly. "He doesn't know you can play?"

"He's not around much," Nikos said simply. "I don't play it in front of him."

"Why?"

Nikos laughed, but it sounded sad. "The only time he'd even care is if the cameras were rolling."

"I'm sorry," I said again. "I didn't mean to—"

"Forget it." He busied himself nestling the bouzouki in a felt-lined case.

I felt like the biggest killjoy ever. "I can go," I offered. "You don't have to quit."

"It's okay." The case closed with a loud click. "I'm done for tonight anyway."

Behind me, Zoe sucked in a breath. I had almost forgotten she was there. It took me a second to switch gears in my head. Zoe hadn't wanted Nikos to find her listening to him play in the first place, but now it was even worse, because it was like she was eavesdropping, too. If Nikos left now, he was sure to see her.

"Oh. Uh . . ." I fumbled for something to say to stop him.

Nikos glanced up. "What?"

"Have you seen Zoe?" I heard her gasp again. "I was coming down to meet her when I heard you playing."

"She was coming here?"

"Yeah. She was going to show me that video game you were talking about yesterday. She's got that one too and she's really good."

"Zoe?"

"Yes, Zoe." At least I guessed she was good, based on the score I saw on the screen the night before. "Don't sound so surprised. She could probably beat you, you know."

He laughed. "How would you know? I thought you didn't know how to play."

"I don't. That's why I'm looking for Zoe."

"I could show you," he offered.

"Oh. Uh, sure." Anything to get him away from the door. Then all Zoe would have to do is pretend to come into the room. She could join us, and she and Nikos could play the video game and sparks would fly and it would be perfect.

But Zoe didn't follow the script. Nikos led me over to the game and booted it up. I thought I could hear Zoe slipping out of the door behind us, so I waited for her to come back in. And I kept on waiting. Zoe never did reappear.

I was so preoccupied listening for her, I'm afraid I wasn't a very good student. Nikos kept trying to explain the characters, the powers, and the levels, but none of it sank in. A) I wasn't really that interested, and B) I was too busy wondering where Zoe went, and how I was going to keep her from running away whenever Nikos got close enough to do something about that crush of hers.

"Maybe we can do this another time?" Nikos asked.

"Yeah. I'm sorry." I yawned for effect. "I didn't realize how tired I was."

"Come on," he said, turning off the game console. "I'll walk you to your cabin."

12

Much later that night, I wrapped up in a blanket and sat out on my private balcony, watching the moonlight skip and pirouette over the water. I had gone to bed hours before, but I couldn't make my mind be quiet long enough to let me sleep.

Scenes from that night kept replaying in my head, from the minute I blew the chat with Logan to the long walk back to my room with Nikos after I had interrupted his jam session and sent Zoe running. How had I developed such a talent for doing and saying the wrong thing?

I had tried to salvage the evening after we left the game room, but I probably only made things worse.

"So have you known Zoe a long time?" I asked Nikos.

He kind of half shrugged and mumbled something I think was "Don't know," but I couldn't be sure.

So I tried again. "How long has she worked on the *Pandora*?"

Nikos's expression became completely unreadable. "Long time, I guess," he said.

He guessed? The *Pandora* was his dad's yacht. How could he not know? Unless . . . I wanted to kick myself. Of course. Nikos said his dad wasn't around much. Maybe Nikos didn't know anything about his dad's yacht because he didn't spend much time here. *Smooth, Cassidy. Real smooth.*

I probably should have shut up about then, but I have this habit of talking too much when a situation gets awkward, so I couldn't turn it off even if I had wanted to.

"Well, she's really nice," I babbled. "You should really get to know her."

"O-kaaay," he said slowly.

"I mean, if you want to."

By that time, we were on the promenade deck, just outside the doors that led into the cabin hallway. We both reached for the handle at the same time, and his hand came down on top of mine. He didn't move his right away, and I didn't want to yank mine back or anything like that, so I did what I do when I can't think of the appropriate response—I laughed.

Which drew the attention of Zoe, who, until that moment, I hadn't seen in the shadows, coming up the steps toward us. She froze for an instant, and then turned around and ran the other way.

I wanted to go after her, but I was afraid I'd just say something stupid. Or worse, tip Nikos off that there was a potential problem. So I just said good night and hurried off to my room.

Now, hours later, I still wondered if I had done the right thing. Maybe I should have tried to explain to Zoe, to let her know I was on her side. Maybe I should have stayed and talked to Nikos.

I had turned to Magus's book of Greek philosophers' quotes looking for an answer, but it only made me more confused. The only quote I could relate to was Socrates, when he said all he knew was that he knew nothing.

Still, another quote stuck in my head that I couldn't stop thinking about. Plato said you could learn more about a person in one hour of play than in a whole year of conversation. So I was on the right track, trying to get Zoe and Nikos to play that video game together, but they didn't cooperate. Maybe it was time to step it up a little. Like tomorrow, when we went wakeboarding.

Whatever it took, I resolved, I had to make sure Zoe went out on that boat with us.

● ● ● ● ●

Travel tip: The Greeks do not like people who are pretentious or standoffish.

CJ ate breakfast with us the next morning, mainly so she could go over the day's itinerary and make sure both Nikos and I knew our lines.

"We can review Cassidy's lines during lesson time this morning," Victoria assured her.

"Nikos will practice as well," Mr. Kouropoulos said.

"Very good." CJ made a little note on her clipboard. "As you can see on the schedule, we will be filming the introduction to the Santorini segment at sundown. For the sake of capturing the moment, we'd like to get it in the can on the first take." Then CJ looked directly at me. "I understand Magus will be taking you out on the boat this morning."

I nodded, and she eyed me critically. "You'd better wear a hat, and plenty of sunscreen. We can't disrupt the shoot for a sunburn. Jacqueline wouldn't be happy about working with pink skin, either."

Nikos didn't get the sunscreen lecture, which was completely unfair. Maybe with his darker skin, CJ figured he never burned. Or if he did, that it wouldn't show up quite as much as it would on me.

I promised CJ I would slather myself in sunscreen, and excused myself from the table. I hadn't seen Zoe yet that morning, and I needed to talk to her.

"Not so fast," Victoria said. "Lessons first."

I groaned. Three hours would never pass so slowly.

Once Victoria finally set me free, I went searching for Zoe. I found her on the main deck, sitting in a lounge chair with a book on her lap. She wasn't reading it, though; she was just staring out at the water.

The way her posture tensed up, I knew she heard me coming, even if she didn't let on that she did.

"Where did you go last night?" I demanded.

She just shrugged and flipped through a couple pages in her book.

"I thought you could come show Nikos how good you are at that game and—"

"He rather see you play, I think," she said sulkily.

"What? Me? No. That wasn't what—"

"He does not see me," she said.

"I thought you didn't *want* him to see you." I mean, wasn't that why she was hiding? But then she looked up at me miserably and I understood. "Oh. You mean, you don't think he notices you?"

She nodded.

"I'm not sure that's true." I scraped a chair up next to hers and sat down. "I saw the way he looked at you yesterday, when we were taking pictures. Zoe, I think he notices you plenty. He just needs to know you notice him."

"But I . . . I cannot . . ."

"I'm not talking about going up to him and telling him

flat out that you like him, but it wouldn't hurt if you talked to him a little more."

"But I—"

"Listen, Magus is taking us out on the boat later. Why don't you come, too?"

Her dark eyes grew wide, and she shook her head. "Oh, no. I could not."

"Sure you could," I insisted. "You're done with your jobs, right? Otherwise you wouldn't be up here reading. Is there something else you have to do?"

"Well . . . no, but—"

"So come with us. It would be perfect."

"But . . ." She started to protest again, but she hesitated. It was the hesitation that gave her away. She really wanted to go.

"We'll ask your mom," I said, standing. "I'm sure she'll say yes. Come on."

Zoe allowed me to drag her along to the galley (which is what a kitchen is called on a yacht, Nikos informed me). I figured it would be a pretty good bet that we'd find Theia Alexa there, and I was right. I was also right about her saying yes to Zoe going on the boat. Zoe's eyes lit right up, but still, she hesitated.

"I must get my suit," she said.

"I'll come with you." Not that I wanted to be smothering or anything, but after she took off on me last night, I

wasn't taking any chances that she would get cold feet again
and not show up.

The cabin Zoe shared with her mother was on the lower
deck. It didn't look like mine at all. For one thing, there was
no balcony—just a couple of round, brass-framed porthole
windows. That right there made the room feel smaller. And
then there was the fact that it *was* smaller. No king-size
bed. No desk. No couch. No big-screen TV. Instead, it was
simple and utilitarian, with built-in drawers and cupboards
along one wall, and two bunk-size beds with a small, connecting nightstand against the other. That was it. Just this
small room for two people. The door to their bathroom
stood partially open, and I could see that it was less than a
third the size of the one I had all to myself. It made me feel
more than a little guilty.

Zoe opened one of the small drawers against the wall
and dug through it for a moment before pulling out a blue-
striped tankini top and a pair of board shorts. "Just one
minute. I change."

She slipped into the tiny bathroom and I waited. I wasn't
trying to be nosy. I really wasn't. But as I was standing there,
I couldn't help but notice small things about the room. Like
the pink, fuzzy pillow on one of the beds that reminded me
of my own blue, fuzzy, travel pillow. Or the line of photos
along the ledge above the drawers.

I stepped closer. Awww. Theia Alexa was sentimental. It looked like all the pictures were of Zoe, at various ages. There she was with long pigtails, wearing what looked like a school uniform. Here she was in a black tank swimsuit with a collection of medals hanging from striped ribbons around her neck. Another picture showed her surrounded by other girls in black tank suits. A team. Zoe must be a competitive swimmer. And . . . I stepped even closer. Was that Zoe as a baby? It was hard to tell.

The woman in the picture was definitely Theia Alexa, standing on a pier with a handsome, dark-haired man. Zoe's father, I guessed. Theia Alexa was holding a curly-haired toddler on her hip. The toddler was wearing a sailor-collared romper and had Zoe's expressive eyes. Behind them all . . . it was the *Pandora*. Wow. Theia Alexa must have worked on the yacht for a long time. No wonder Zoe seemed to have a connection to it. She must have been here a lot as she was growing up.

I don't have body-image issues. At least, I didn't think I did. But when Zoe came out of the bathroom, all I could think of was that I was going to look like I was about five next to her.

She'd always been wearing a uniform or an apron before, so it hadn't been that noticeable, but now that I had pegged her as a competitive swimmer, I recognized the athlete's build. Plus, she didn't need any of my stupid push-up bras. She had such a perfect figure, she looked like she could be a model.

Suddenly, I wasn't so sure I wanted to go out on the boat after all. But then, this outing wasn't about me. And if I didn't look quite as good as Zoe did, that worked out well for matchmaking, didn't it? I decided I would go along, if only to prove to Nikos that he should be giving Zoe a second look.

Zoe came with me back to my room, where I slipped into my own bathroom to change into my swimsuit. For a cover-up, I pulled on my favorite pair of jean shorts, trying not to look in the mirror so I wouldn't be tempted to compare myself to Zoe again. I gave myself a mini pep talk, took a deep breath, and opened the door.

To my surprise, Zoe looked at me with the same kind of self-conscious evaluation as I had given her in her room. When she saw that I recognized what she was doing, she gave a kind of half shrug and smiled her beautiful smile.

"I like your . . . shorts," she said hesitantly, gesturing to her own board shorts, as if I wouldn't know what she was talking about otherwise. "I cannot wear the jeans like you do," she said wistfully. "My thighs are too-big big muscles."

Now that she mentioned it, she really did have muscular thighs, but they weren't too big. She had broad shoulders, too, I guess, which probably came from the swimming. But as far as I was concerned, she looked perfect.

"They're not too big," I said. "Really."

She shuffled a little and adjusted the hem on one of the legs of her shorts. "They are big," she said. "I like the skinny jeans, but all are for me too tight in the thighs. They are only straight from hip to the ankle."

"I know!" I said. "Who are the manufacturers making those for anyway? Because, hello. Girls are not shaped straight up and down."

She laughed. "You are true."

We stood there still smiling after the laughter faded, but it didn't feel awkward. I had never known what it was like to have a girlfriend because we never stayed in one place long enough for me to get to know anyone that way. But if I had, I imagined this was what it would be like. Feeling comfortable enough to talk about random stuff. Sharing a laugh. Talking about boys.

On impulse I said, "Hey, do you want to see a picture of Logan? I have one on my computer."

"I would like that," Zoe said.

I rushed to the desk and turned on the computer. "It's only his chat icon, but at least you can see what he looks like." I opened the chat connection and stood back. "He's that one, right there." I pointed toward the screen, but it wasn't really necessary. She'd know that Logan's icon was the one that was *not* a picture of my mom and dad.

"Very . . . handsome," Zoe said. "He is nice boy?"

"He's my best friend," I told her.

"Where he is from?" she asked.

"He's Irish. His dad works for the network that does my mom and dad's show."

"He travels with you?"

I nodded. No need to explain the whole mess to her.

"You are very lucky," she said.

"I think so. I—"

Just then, the phone sound rang from my computer. I jumped and my heart started doing ninety. Logan must have been online and saw me sign in. Zoe could meet him!

But then it registered that Logan's icon wasn't lit up. "Oh," I said, trying not to sound too disappointed. "It's my mom and dad."

"Do you want me to . . ." Zoe gestured toward the door.

"No. Stay here. We have to get out to the boat, so it will have to be quick."

I clicked on my mom and dad's icon, and my mom's face popped up on my screen. "Oh! Hi, sweetie! We thought maybe you were out."

"Hi, Mom." I said.

"Davidson!" my mom yelled over her shoulder. "She's on!" Then she turned back to me. "How are you doing? I see you're in your swimsuit. Are you going swimming?"

I settled into the chair in front of the computer and adjusted the angle of the webcam so that I was centered in the little picture of myself I could see at the top left corner of the screen. "Yeah. We're going out in the boat in just a few minutes."

"Boat?" she asked. "Aren't you already on the boat?"

"They have a speedboat that docks right into the yacht," I said. "Isn't that cool?"

"It certainly sounds . . . cool," she said, but she sounded unsure. "A *speed*boat, you say? Is this for the show? I didn't see anything about that in the outline for the special. . . ."

"We have some time off today, so we're going out before the shoot to go wakeboarding and—"

"To go what?" She scooted closer to her computer and her eyes dropped to the keys. I could tell by the *clack, clack, clack* she was typing something. Probably googling wakeboarding. Her eyes got a little wider. Yup.

"It is very fun," Zoe offered.

"Zoe says it's fun," I said.

"Oh? Who is Zoe?"

"She's my friend who works here on the yacht." I motioned for her. "Come here, Zoe. Say hi to my mom."

Zoe came around to my side of the desk, and I scooted over so she could sit on the chair next to me, facing the webcam. *"Yiasou,"* she said, giving a little wave. "Hello."

"Well, hello, Zoe," my mom said. "It's nice to meet you."

"Nice to meet you," Zoe replied.

"You'd like Zoe's mom, Mom," I said. "She's the cook here on board and she's fantastic. She could show you how to cook real Greek cuisine."

"I hope I get the chance to meet her someday."

"How was the pig?" I asked.

"The pig?"

"Logan said you were roasting a pig last night."

"Oh, yes." She nodded. "He said he spoke to you."

I wanted to ask her what else he said, but I decided against it. At least I knew he was talking about me.

"You two have such complementary coloring," Mom mused.

I blinked in surprise. Wow. Complementary coloring? Was that her way of saying Logan and I looked good together? Did she even know I liked him that way?

My mind drifted a little, imagining how the two of us would look as a couple. He had dark, nearly black hair and indescribable deep green eyes while I was blonde with what my dad called "baby blues." So, yeah, I guess you could say we complemented each other. But it was still weird to hear my mom say so.

And then I noticed the webcam picture on my computer screen of Zoe and me sitting side-by-side, and I had to laugh. Her black, curly hair, dark eyes, and olive skin next to my blonde hair, blue eyes, and peachy-tan coloring was a complementary contrast. I was kind of relieved to realize my mom probably wasn't talking about Logan and me because that would just be weird.

"Where is your appliance?" Mom asked.

I stopped laughing. "My palate expander?" I asked.

"Yes. Where is it?"

Oh. I still hadn't put it back in. Oops. "It's, um, in the bathroom."

"Be sure to remember to wear it. Zoe, you can remind her so she doesn't forget, okay?"

"Mom . . ." I couldn't believe she asked Zoe to do that. "I have to go," I said. "We're supposed to be meeting at the boat."

Mom turned from the screen again. "Davidson!" she yelled. "You're going to miss her!"

I could hear Dad's voice in the background. "Hold on!" Some stomping, some shuffling, and then Dad's face appeared on the screen next to Mom's. "Sorry, Cassie-bug."

"Don't call me that," I grumbled.

He cheerfully ignored me. "How's it going? Are you having a good time? We saw your blog posts. Very nice. When can we expect to see an update?"

"Tonight," I assured him. "After the shoot."

"And who is with you?" He asked.

"That's Cassidy's new friend, Zoe," Mom said—as if I couldn't answer for myself. "She works on the yacht."

Zoe's smile lost some of its sparkle when she said that, and suddenly I felt bad for having introduced Zoe that way, as if working on the yacht was her identity. Why couldn't I have just said Zoe was my friend and leave it at that?

I quickly reminded my mom and dad that I had to go.

"You be careful," Mom said.

"I will," I promised. "I love you."

"Love you, too, Cassie-bug," Dad said.

"Palate expander!" Mom reminded me.

I signed off before they could embarrass me further.

"They are very nice," Zoe said. "Do you miss them?"

"Sometimes," I admitted.

"I miss my father sometimes, too," she said. "He work in the city so he cannot sail often with us."

Sail with them? Maybe Mr. Kouropoulos let Zoe's dad come with them when he wasn't working. That was pretty cool, I supposed.

"What does your dad do?" I asked.

Zoe bit the edge of her lip. "It is past time," she said. "We should go."

Oh, the boat! "Just a minute." I closed down the computer. "I have to put in my stupid expander."

In the bathroom, I pulled it out of the case and tried to click it into place in my mouth, but it was too tight. I had to jiggle it to make it fit, which didn't make my teeth happy.

Zoe glanced up when I stepped out of the bathroom, massaging my upper gums through my lips. "What is wrong?" she asked.

"It's nothing. I forgot to wear this thing for a couple daysh and now it'sh tight."

"It hurts you?" she asked.

I tried to shrug it off and ignore the discomfort. "It'sh fine," I lied. "We better get going."

Nikos was already on the boat with

Magus when Zoe and I got there. "About time!" he said.
"Victoria went back to get you."

"My mom and dad called," I told him. "I couldn't get
away."

Zoe was hanging back, so I took her hand and pulled
her forward with me. Nikos lifted his dark glasses when he
saw her, and watched us climb on board.

"*Yiasou,*" he said to Zoe.

"*Yiasou,*" she said softly in return.

They were both being shy. It was adorable. I wanted to
smile at them, but my mouth was already aching from the
palate expander. I kind of grimaced instead and sank down
on one of the seats.

"There you are!" Victoria hurried across the deck to the boat. "I just went to your room to look for you."

She was wearing a wide-brimmed hat and sunglasses. I remembered guiltily that I had promised CJ I would wear a hat, too. Oops. "Shorry," I told Victoria. "Mom and Dad called."

She climbed into the boat and sat next to me. "Do you need some of this?" She handed me a bottle of SPF 40 sunscreen. Of course she would be prepared.

I rubbed some over my arms and legs and some on my face. My mouth was full-on throbbing by then, so I had to wash off my hands so I could massage my gums again.

Victoria got that concerned big-sister look on her face. "What's wrong?" she asked.

"It'sh my shtupid palate exshpander."

"Ah." I'd left the thing off before—she'd been through the drama with me on more than one occasion. My mouth would be sore for a day or so before it got back to normal. "Not worth the neglect, is it?"

"I didn't want to wear it in front of the camerash."

She considered that for a moment and nodded. "Well, perhaps you can take it out for your segments, but then you should put it back in. I can remind you if you like."

"No, thanksh," I said glumly.

"Here." She handed me a hunter-orange life vest. "We need to put these on. Mandatory."

I slipped it over my head and tightened the straps as

Magus took his place at the front of the boat. "Everyone is ready?" he asked.

We all gave him the thumbs-up.

He revved the motor. "Here we go!"

Over the whine of the engine and the rush of air in our ears, Victoria explained that Magus had to take us out far enough that we'd be well outside the ferry and shipping lanes. The water had taken on the darkest shade of blue I'd seen yet, and I realized from my water lesson with Nikos the day before that it must be deeper there.

By the time we slowed, the yacht was just a white dot in the distance and the islands floated like little specks on the horizon. Magus steered the boat in a lazy circle until it idled still in the water. "So," he said, facing us. "Who will go first?"

Nikos, of course, jumped up to volunteer. He chose his board—black and silver and shaped like a stubby snowboard—and moved to the back of the boat to sit on the swim deck and strap it on. After he dropped into the water, it took him a few minutes to get situated, and then Zoe threw him the line. "Watch!" he called to Zoe and me. "I'll show you how it's done."

Magus waited until Nikos signaled, and then started forward, slowly at first and then picking up speed. I watched nervously as the rope tow behind the boat straightened, stretched, and grew taut, pulling Nikos up out of the water. He started to stand up, but then the rope pulled him right over and he face-planted in the waves. White, foamy water spouted up and over his head as he was dragged behind the boat.

"Let go!" Zoe yelled through cupped hands, even though he probably couldn't have heard her through all the rushing water in his ears. She giggled and turned to me. "This is *not* how it is done."

Finally, Nikos released his grip on the rope, and Magus brought the boat around to idle beside him again.

"You want to try again?" Magus asked.

Nikos was too out of breath to answer, so he just raised his hand and nodded yes. Zoe pulled the rope into the boat and then threw him the handle again. He caught it and brought his board up so that the edge was sticking up out of the water.

"Tuck in tight!" Magus yelled. "Do not fight the boat!"

Nikos clenched his jaw and signaled that he was ready again. He did better that time, pulling up from the water cleanly, and managing to keep the board on top of the wake for a few seconds before it sliced downward and he wiped out. At least this time he remembered to let go of the rope.

Magus chuckled as he brought the boat around again. "Again?" he called.

Nikos nodded once more and leaned back in the water, letting the life jacket keep him afloat until the rope was thrown to him again.

"Toes up!" Magus shouted.

Nikos waved tiredly.

One more time, Magus eased the boat forward. Nikos rocked back on his heels, keeping the board above the wake. He pulled up out of the water, but then rode for almost a full minute in a crouch, as if he was afraid to stand up. Once he finally pulled himself up, he had a decent run—maybe four or five minutes—before Magus turned the boat, and Nikos hit the wake wrong. He tumbled sideways with a spectacular splash.

I thought maybe Nikos would be upset that he had fallen so many times or that he'd had so much trouble getting started, but he was laughing as he climbed into the boat.

"Woo! That was awesome!" He shook the water from his curls. "Who's next?"

I sank back against the cushions. "I've never done it before. I think I need to watch shome more."

Zoe stood up. "I will go."

Watching Zoe wakeboard was an entirely different experience than watching poor Nikos. The first time she signaled Magus that she was ready, she really and truly was. The rope pulled tight, and she rose from the water like Aphrodite. She shifted her weight gracefully and turned so that she stood on the board, holding the rope by her front hip. She made it look easy.

I imagined the sound of the clunk Nikos's jaw made as

it hit the floor. He was staring at her as if he'd never seen her before. Bingo.

Zoe rode for a while—I lost track of how long—zig-zagging over the wake, even turning backward a couple of times. She didn't fall to finish her run. Oh, no. She simply signaled Magus, let go of the rope, and sank slowly into the water.

When she climbed back onto the boat, Nikos couldn't get to her quick enough. "Where did you learn how to do that? Show me how you did that turn."

She tucked her chin shyly, but smiled and answered all his questions in her soft, direct way. She demonstrated how he could move his weight on the board for better control, and he imitated her moves as much as he could.

"How long have you been doing this?" Nikos wanted to know.

Zoe shrugged slightly. "Since I have been little," she said. "We would come out on this boat very often, before . . ." She ran her hand over the railing like she was stroking a kitten. Lovingly, almost longingly.

Nikos slid a quick look toward Victoria and me. "Yeah." He cleared his throat. "Uh . . . can you show me how you spin like that? I always bite it the moment I let go of the rope with one hand."

She demonstrated again, and he followed her lead, watching intently as she explained the release.

I was glad to see that Nikos wasn't one of those guys who got put off because a girl was better at something than he was. I once read in one of those "how to get a guy" magazine articles that guys have very fragile egos, and they don't like girls who can outplay them. I always thought that was stupid. Who wanted to be with someone who always had to be better than you were in order to be happy?

Nikos may have acted like he had a king-size ego, but in those moments on the boat I could see he was more interested in what Zoe could do than he was in what *he* could do, and that made me like him for Zoe even more.

Before you wonder about it too much, yes, I tried to wakeboard, too. I managed to stand up twice, but I didn't stay up for very long. Still, like all good things, it was fun while it lasted.

> *Happiness depends on ourselves.*
> —**Aristotle**

Our shoot that evening was on the island of Santorini. After the afternoon on the boat, my arms and legs felt like deflated balloons filled with wet sand. I pretty much had to drag myself to the makeup chair and wanted to fall asleep sitting there.

"What have you done to your face?" Jacqueline demanded when she started in to work on me. "How to you expect me to achieve the same skin tone you had this morning if you insist on cooking yourself like meat under the sun?"

"I wore sunscreen," I protested.

"You should have worn a hat! Just look at this mess!" She turned my head from side to side and *tsked*. "I'll have to use a green underbase. Do not do this again."

I promised her I wouldn't and she set about dabbing and rubbing and powdering my face until she was satisfied it wouldn't ruin the continuity of the filming.

Since we would be docking in Oia, she didn't need to put my hair in the annoying rollers, but part of our segment was going to be filmed on the yacht and she was afraid of a breeze messing up my hair, so she had me wear a headband to keep it under control.

Five minutes before we were supposed to show up for the sound check, Nikos dropped into the chair next to mine. "Why didn't you tell me about Zoe before?" he asked.

"What did you want me to tell?"

"She's so . . . and when she got up on that board . . . and those eyes!" He sighed and fell against the back of the chair. "Did you know she can almost beat me at arm wrestling?"

I gave him a sideways glance. "Almost?"

"All right, she pinned me. But she was *holding my hand*!"

"So you like her."

Suddenly, his face turned serious. "You can't tell any-one."

"Who would I tell?"

"Quiet. You two are giving me a headache." Jacqueline had finished with me and moved over to Nikos's chair. She grabbed his jaw and turned his head so that his face was to the sun. "Close your eyes," she ordered.

When he had been properly powdered and his curls tamed with a dime-sized dollop of gel, she released him.

"Who don't you want me to tell?" I asked him again.

"We better hurry," he said. "The sun is dipping low already and they haven't even wired us yet."

And then he ran off, evading my question.

14

You've probably seen pictures of Oia on postcards or travel posters. It's one of the towns on Santorini built right along the top edge of a cliff. All the buildings, the walls, the stairs—everything in the town is painted white. No, I take that back. Not everything. The doors and shutters and handrails are all painted in bright, cheerful colors. And the domes of the churches are blue like the Aegean Sea.

When I was reading my lines for the Santorini segment, I learned that the island Oia is on is actually the rim of a caldera that was formed thousands of years ago. In case you're wondering what a caldera is, it's a big, basin-shaped hole in the ground that's usually made when land collapses around a volcano after it erupts. The islands of Santorini are on the rim of the caldera, with thousand-foot cliffs that look over the sunken center.

As we sailed toward Santorini, the white towns built on the edges of those cliffs made the rim look like it was topped with snow. I stood at the railing on the yacht and watched the cities appear as we got closer. The sound guy came to finish connecting my mic, but I didn't move. All I could do was stare at Oia, the closest city. This was the view I always imagined when I thought of Greece. Actually seeing it in front of me was like a dream.

"Okay, listen up." CJ said. "The sun is setting so we only have time to run through this once."

My dream bubble disappeared in a "poof!" and I turned to listen to her directions.

"When we're through with your lines on the *Pandora*, we'll head into town for the Atlantis segment. Ready? Let's go!"

Nikos looked into the camera as if he knew each viewer on the other side of the lens personally. "At one time in its history, Santorini was a single island."

"Over the space of thousands of years," I continued, "a series of earthquakes and volcanic eruptions caused the center of the island to sink, leaving behind a group of smaller islands. This is why scholars guess Santorini could actually be the home of the lost city of Atlantis."

"Cut!" yelled CJ. "Cassidy, the line is, '*some* scholars guess.' Not all. Some. Do you think you can get that right?"

The tone in her voice made my chest cave in. I wasn't used to being yelled at. I knew a professional would suck it up and try again, but it stung. "Sorry," I said in a small voice.

CJ didn't answer, but turned to the crew and yelled, "Let's go again!"

Nikos found my hand and squeezed it before starting his line again.

I squeezed his hand back. As far as I was concerned, Nikos had just scored major points. I hoped Zoe had seen how sweet he could be. I smiled into the camera as I corrected my flub. "This is why *some* scholars guess Santorini could be the home of the lost city of Atlantis."

"Nobody knows about that for sure," Nikos said, "but what they can tell you is that Santorini is home to some of the most beautiful sights in the world."

"I'm Cassidy."

"And I'm Nikos."

"Welcome to Santorini!" we said together, sweeping our arms out toward Oia.

"And . . . cut!" CJ said. "Okay, that was good. Now let's get just a few frames of you two standing with the sun setting behind you. Gabe, are you getting this? Good. Now turn so that we've got the city in the background. Smile, smile. And that's good."

She turned to the rest of the crew. "Okay, everyone, pack it up. We'll reconvene in the city in thirty minutes. Chop-chop!"

Victoria brought each of us a bottled water. "Just two takes," she said. "Not bad."

Yeah, tell CJ that. I was still stinging from the way she yelled at me.

Nikos unscrewed the lid to his water. "Where's Zoe?" he asked. "Is she coming into town with us?"

"I think she's going in with her mum," Victoria said.

He deflated. "Oh."

I shouldn't have been so happy to see his disappointment, but I was proud of myself. Just two days ago, Nikos didn't even look at Zoe. Now he didn't want to let her out of his sight. I had mad matchmaking skills.

There's a small road that winds up to Oia from the Ammoudi port, but Mr. Kouropolous suggested that we walk. It wasn't far, he said, and he thought we would enjoy it. CJ and the crew took a van. The rest of us started with the steps. Two hundred and fourteen steps. I know because I counted. It was a hike, but the view of the sea and the cliffs on the way up was amazing. Now that the sun had set, lights from the boats and yachts below reflected like watery fairy lanterns in the harbor. Above us, the white city was lit so that it practically glowed.

It wasn't until we were about halfway up the stairs that

I realized there might be another reason why he suggested we walk. A group of photographers crowded down the steps toward us. "Over here!" "Just one smile!" "This way!"

Magus immediately moved Nikos and me behind him as we continued up the stairs and Victoria positioned herself right next to me, but Mr. Kouropolous seemed to forget we were even there. He played to the paparazzi the rest of the way up until CJ met us at the top of the stairs and shooed the photographers away.

Once they were gone, Mr. Kouropolous lost interest in staying with the group and wandered off. I'm not even exactly sure when he left. All I know is at the beginning he was with us, but about midway through he was gone. One of the crew members told us he said he'd meet us back at port.

If it bothered Nikos that his dad had ditched us again, he didn't say anything. Out loud anyway. But I caught the way his jaw tightened when he scanned the streets around us, and the tiniest tug of a frown when he saw for himself his dad was gone. Still, he was able to smile and turn on the charm for the camera so that you'd never know anything was wrong. I admired his professionalism. And yet I wondered how much it covered what Nikos felt inside.

We worked straight through dinnertime. I'm pretty sure somewhere in that agreement we signed, there was something about the child talent being fed. But CJ kept reminding us that we had only one night in Santorini, so if we didn't get the shots they needed, they were going to have to throw the entire segment out.

"I'd offer to go grab something," Victoria told me, "but I'm not allowed to leave you during filming. As soon as you finish up, we'll eat, I promise."

"One more time, from the top!" CJ cried.

With the promise of food waiting for us, Nikos and I plowed through the segment. What we were basically doing was debating the possibility that the legend of the lost city of Atlantis was referring to the eruptions on the island of Santorini. The lost city, some people believed, was actually the sunken center of the caldera. Our lines were long and wordy, and it was kind of hard to keep the fake perkiness in our voices after about the tenth take, but finally, we did it to CJ's strict standard, and we were released. Only not in time to stop for something to eat before we had to go back to the *Pandora*.

"I'll have a talk with the network," Victoria vowed. "This is simply unacceptable."

"It's okay," I told her. "I bet we can find something in the kitchen when we get back."

That wasn't really the point, and I knew it, but I also knew my mom and dad would freak if the network told them the production company wasn't living up to their part of the agreement. I didn't want Victoria to make that phone call.

● ● ● ● ●

The moment we got back onto the yacht Nikos, Victoria, and I made a beeline for the galley.

"There's probably leftovers from lunch," I said hopefully.

"I'd settle for bread and cheese," Nikos said.

Victoria stopped. "Do you smell that?"

Theia Alexa had beaten us to the galley. She looked startled when the three of us came walking into her space.

Behind her mom, Zoe glanced up from where she was dicing onions. I couldn't help but notice the way she and Nikos looked at each other. Sparks were flying all the way across the room.

"We're sorry to intrude," Victoria said, "but the kids never got a chance to eat while we were in town. I was hoping we could scrounge something up in here."

"Of course!" Theia Alexa said. "And you are right on time. Tonight I try to prepare tomato *keftedes* like the ones we taste in town. Santorini is known for their tomato *keftedes*, and I want to discover the recipe before I lose the flavor up here." She tapped her head with the handle of her spoon.

"I volunteer to be a taste tester," Nikos said.

I nudged him. "You would."

Zoe hid a smile and brought her cutting board over to where her mother was mixing a bowl full of red goop. (Hey—that's what it looked like. But it smelled good.) As she stirred in the onions Zoe had chopped, I tried to see if I could identify the smell of the other spices the way Nikos had with the moussaka. Nope. Except maybe for mint. But whatever else was in there made my mouth water.

Theia Alexa dipped the tip of her pinkie finger into the mixture and tasted the result. "Hmmm . . . Zoe?"

Zoe daintily dipped in her finger and tasted the batter. "More salt, I think."

Nikos leaned forward, but Theia Alexa pulled the bowl closer to her. "You will wait until they are done."

I couldn't help but laugh, and he slugged my arm. Lightly. Such a gentleman.

Theia Alexa sprinkled in more salt, and then dropped the sticky mixture by spoonfuls into in a shallow pan to fry. The cooking *keftedes* made the whole kitchen smell fabulous . . . and my stomach grumble even more.

I don't know if it was the wait, or because I was hungry, or if the *keftedes* really were that good, but I couldn't get enough of them. And I wasn't the only one. Nikos and Victoria and I ate the entire batch without stopping.

"You have a half hour until lights out," Victoria told me. "Why don't you and Nikos and Zoe enjoy the fresh air, and I'll help Theia Alexa clean up."

We didn't have to be told twice. As fast as we could go, we ran out to the deck. In the moonlight, we walked around and talked about nonsense stuff . . . like soccer. (Nikos was a huge fan of the Panathinaikos, and Zoe loved the Olympiakos. From what I could tell, those two teams were major rivals.) They were so into their argument and recitation of stats that I don't think either of them even remembered I was still there. It reminded me of when Logan and Mateo got going about soccer in Spain. I could have been on the moon for all they knew.

Still, I couldn't help but smile. My job as Eros was complete. I decided to bow out so they could be alone together. "I should go in now," I told them, backing away.

Remember that panicked-deer look? Now both of them had it. They stared at me, wide-eyed, making little gestures with their heads that I'm pretty sure meant they didn't want me to leave. What were they—afraid of being alone together?

Yes.

Believe it or not, even though you could see that each of them had it bad for the other, I think they were afraid of running out of things to say, or saying the wrong thing, or freezing up, or whatever. Because it continued like that for the next two days. Wherever they were, I had to be there, too, to act as a kind of buffer.

I learned very quickly what is meant when people talk about a "third wheel." They went out on the boat, played video games, strolled along the deck, Nikos played his bouzouki for Zoe . . . all with me tagging along.

I didn't mind so much; it was fun hanging out, just the

three of us. But I didn't understand why both of them were so worried about keeping it secret.

"Maybe they're just shy," Logan said when I told him about it during one of our online chats.

"I don't know," I said. "Why would they be?"

Although, I guessed in a way it made sense; if we ever told anyone, if we ever talked about it openly, they would each have to own the fact that they liked each other. Once it was out there, the chance for rejection became a reality. It was much easier just to let things slide and hope that the other person liked you as much as you liked them without actually confronting them about it. I knew; I was doing the exact same thing by not talking to anyone about how much I liked Logan.

"Okay," Logan said. "Then maybe there's something else going on. I'll bet you're going to snoop until you find out what it is, aren't you?"

"I resent that," I sniffed, pretending to be hurt. "I never snoop."

Logan laughed. "Right. You won't be able to leave it alone."

15

On day six of the cruise, our shoot was scheduled on the island of Milos.

"We should see if Zoe can come," I told Nikos as we sat in the makeup chairs.

Nikos slid a quick glance over to where his dad was talking on his cell phone and then he shook his head. "I think she said she had to help out here."

"We're only going to be onshore for three hours," I said. "I'll bet Theia Alexa could do without her for that long."

But Zoe said the same thing as Nikos when I asked her. "I must prepare the dinner."

"You have to come," I said. "We'll be going to the beach after the shoot."

She just shrugged—rather sadly, I thought. "I can't."

I dropped the subject after that, but it didn't stop me from wondering. For two people who wanted to be together, they sure were quick about giving in.

Another swarm of paparazzi were waiting to swoop in on us when we docked in Milos. By that time, I should have been used to it, but seeing all those cameras still gave me a little thrill, even though I knew by then that it wasn't me they were coming to see.

I will say something for them; they sure brought out the best in Mr. Kouropoulos. He could be reclusive and cranky on the yacht, but as soon as the cameras appeared, suddenly he was Prince Charming.

Nikos's mood changed in front of the cameras, too. He would be timid around his dad on board the yacht, but bring on the paparazzi, and he'd turn into his dad's mini-me. All of a sudden he became confident and cocky, the true "Greek Romeo"—just like the fan magazines said.

I guess I probably changed a little in front of the cameras, too. It was fun to act like a diva once in a while. But I wasn't in the mood to ham it up when we got to Milos. I was too bummed that Zoe wouldn't be coming with us— and curious why neither she nor Nikos even asked to find out if she could.

Victoria took my elbow as we walked along the pier to

the waiting limo bus. "Don't forget to smile," she reminded me.

I automatically turned on all one hundred watts, but only until I had climbed onto the bus and the door closed. As we drove away, I watched through the tinted glass as the yacht and the pier and the pack of paparazzi grew smaller in the distance, and I couldn't help but think about Zoe, left behind.

"Cassidy," Victoria said, "are you feeling well?" She pressed the back of her hand to my forehead.

"Oh, no. No." CJ bent forward in her seat to peer at me. "Let's not get sick. We don't have time for illness."

"I'm not sick," I said. "It's just . . . I left something behind on the *Pandora*."

I tried to catch Nikos's eye when I said that, but he just stared at the floor mats at his feet.

"Well, we don't have time for retrieving forgotten items, either," CJ said. "We're running late as it is."

"It's okay," I said, still looking at Nikos, "I'll be sure to bring it next time."

He wouldn't look up, but I could see a flush creep across his olive cheeks.

Because the filming of our next segment took place on a rocky field that sloped down toward the water, the sea breeze was a bit of a challenge. First of all, it kept blowing my hair into my face. Jacqueline finally had to pull my hair back and shellac it in place with hair spray. Then the wind distorted our voices, so the sound guys had to fit our mics with special furry windscreen covers. And because all that took so long, the sun had moved, and the lighting guys had to shift all the screens.

Through it all, Nikos and I were expected to stand on our marks and keep smiling in case anyone wanted to take some "candid" behind-the-scenes stills. I heard somewhere that it takes more muscles to frown than to smile, but I can tell you, even with minimal muscle usage, my cheeks were beginning to hurt. At least my teeth had stopped aching from my stupid palate expander.

"You could have at least asked if she could come along," I told Nikos through a broad, cheek-burning smile.

He flashed a toothy grin at me. "Who?"

"You know who," I said pleasantly. "Zoe."

"You don't get it." Nikos practically laughed. "Zoe is—"

"All right, people," CJ yelled. "Let's try it again from the top. Ready? And, action!"

Nikos didn't miss a beat, but took the smile thing down a couple notches, looked directly into the camera, and launched into his lines. "You probably know her as the lady with no arms. The Romans called her Venus de Milo. But here on the island of Milos, she is known as Aphrodite, the goddess of love." I was surprised he didn't choke on that last part.

"The statue of Aphrodite of Milos was found here"—I swept my arm to encompass the field, the sloping hillside, and the ancient stone amphitheater at the bottom—"nearly two hundred years ago by a local farmer plowing his field."

I'm proud to say that we got the entire segment down in just four takes. Not quite as good as the bit on the boat coming into Santorini, but this segment was longer, so I thought we weren't too bad, considering. I even forgot to be angry at Nikos for not trying to include Zoe in our excursion. Well, almost forgot. Until we went to the beach after the shoot, and I couldn't help but think how much she would have loved swimming with us.

Remember how I told you that the sunset at Santorini was beyond amazing? You should have seen the one we saw tonight from Sarakiniko Beach on the island of Milos.

This beach was like nothing you've ever seen before. The lava rocks surrounding it are as white as chalk and have been worn smooth from years of weather and water. There's a narrow inlet through the rocks that forms a small beach with sand like vanilla sugar, and turquoise water.

But the amazing part was when the sun sank into the horizon and cast a sunset glow over everything. Those white rocks actually looked orange. I'm posting the pictures, but it was even more spectacular in—

A soft knocking startled me from my blog entry. I glanced at the time on my computer: 9:52. Eight minutes until lights-out. I hurried to answer the door. As I hoped, Zoe stood in the hallway. I looked both ways and then hurried her inside.

"I looked for you when we got back," I told her. "Where did you go?"

Her secretive smile told me the answer was going to be good. "Well, don't just stand there. Come tell me about it!"

"Nikos found me," she said.

"Oh, he did. And . . . ?"

She closed her eyes, remembering, I guessed, judging from her smile. "We walk around the deck, talking about many things. I forget some of the words because . . ." She looked at me, and I suddenly understood the meaning of "starry-eyed." "He hold my hand! All I can think of is my hand in his and . . . the happy energy."

I liked the way she put it, "the happy energy." "That's exactly what it's like when I talk with Logan," I told her. "Like I want to jump, to shout. Like I could bounce off walls. I just have so much happy inside that it wants to burst out."

"Yes!" she said. "Like it want to come out and fill the room."

"Like you want to sing!"

"La! La! La!"

We fell back against the cushions and laughed. I was so happy for Zoe. And for Nikos. And for me, because I'd never had a friend I could talk with about boys before. No one I could laugh with like that.

I was so happy when I went to bed that night; I was still smiling. Everything had worked out perfectly. I was completely content.

But fortunes change.

The next morning, I woke up to my cell phone ringing. I thought it was my alarm and fumbled to turn it off before I realized it wasn't the alarm ringtone. It was the incoming call one I had chosen for my mom and dad. I sat up in bed, suddenly very awake, a cold wave rolling through my stomach.

Calling on an international cell phone is expensive. I've gotten that lecture only about a million times. That's why I talk to my mom and dad online. They wouldn't call on the phone unless it was important. And knowing my parents, any good news could wait until I was online. Which could mean only one thing. They weren't calling with good news.

I answered hesitantly. "Hello?"

"Cassidy. Did we wake you?" It was Dad. Even with the distance and the feedback in the cell reception, I could hear the tight tone in his voice.

"Dad? What's wrong?"

"We just received a call from the network," he said.

My mind raced. The way he said it sounded ominous, but I couldn't think of anything I had done that would make the network—and, as a result, my dad—angry. "Okay," I said slowly.

"Do you recall our discussion about Facebook?" he asked.

Facebook? Now I was really confused. "Um, yes. You said I couldn't make an account until I was fourteen and only then with the network's approval."

"Then could you explain," Mom said, "how your picture, along with Nikos Kouropoulos, is being passed around the Facebook site?" She must have been on an extension or sitting right by Dad.

"What?" I said. "I don't know what . . . oh." Suddenly, I remembered that afternoon on the deck. Nikos with his camera. *We should take our own pictures,* he had said. *I could post them on my Facebook page.* "It wasn't my account," I said weakly.

"It's not just about an account," Dad said. "We discussed the need to control the kind of exposure you are subjected to. That means no content on social media without our approval."

"I didn't post the pictures," I said. As if that would make a difference.

"Cassidy." Mom's tone was stern. "We have placed a lot of trust in you by allowing you to go on this trip. We do not expect you to disregard the rules you have agreed to."

"I seriously didn't mean to disregard anything," I said. "I wasn't even thinking."

"Apparently not," Dad said. "That will have to change."

"Yes, sir."

Travel tip: Mealtimes are for socializing. Expect a great deal of discussion at the table.

The morning only went from bad to worse when I went to breakfast. I knew something was up the moment I saw Mr. Kouropoulos, Victoria, and Nikos sitting together at the table, all straight-backed and unsmiling. It looked as if I was walking into the middle of something, and after the phone call that morning, I figured it was over the Facebook thing. But really? It's not like they were bad pictures or anything. Plus, Nikos didn't know anything about my rules or agreements. He shouldn't be in trouble.

I was just debating if I should jump in and defend Nikos, or duck back down the stairs and come back later, when Mr. Kouropoulos glanced up and saw me. Too late.

"Ah. There you are," he said. "Not an early riser, I see."

"Uh," I said brilliantly.

"Come join us," Victoria said, patting the seat next to her.

"Oh. Yes." I realized I had just been standing there staring, and I scurried over to sit by Victoria. Nikos was stirring the food around on his plate and wouldn't look up. Even when I nudged his foot under the table.

"Your itinerary for the day," Victoria said, sliding a sheet of paper toward me. "Courtesy of CJ."

I glanced at it really quickly to make sure she hadn't changed any of the times or anything since I last saw it. We were going to do a shoot on the island of Zakynthos that afternoon, and have a picnic at a place called Shipwreck Beach. Everything still looked the same as I remembered it from the information packet.

It was about that time that Zoe came through the swinging doors from the galley, balancing a tray with four bowls of grapefruit on it. She skillfully worked her way around the table, sliding a bowl from the tray at every place setting and gathering any empty plates.

When she got close to Nikos's chair, she gave him one of her special smiles, but Nikos wouldn't look at her. In fact, Nikos looked everywhere *but* at her. Like he was purposefully avoiding her.

A cloud of confusion crossed her face and her smile quivered a little bit, but she didn't miss a beat at the table. She finished gathering up the empty plates and disappeared back into the kitchen.

What was *that*? I wanted to kick Nikos for real.

But then I noticed the way his dad was watching him. Carefully. Critically. What was going on?

After breakfast, Nikos went off with his dad and left Victoria and me at the table.

"What was that all about?" I asked.

"I'm not sure," Victoria said. "Something to do with Theia Alexa is all I could gather. I came to the table just as she was leaving. She did not look pleased."

"They didn't say anything about it?"

"They hardly said anything at all. It was rather awkward, to say the least. Now hurry up and eat. We have just enough time to get your three hours in before we reach Zakynthos."

16

You'd have thought Victoria would have figured out that I wouldn't be able to concentrate on my lessons when I was preoccupied by something else. But she kept pushing through our allotted time, repeating herself two or three times. I'm not sure how often since I wasn't really listening.

I kept wondering what had been going on at the table that morning. It couldn't have been about the Facebook thing if Theia Alexa was involved. She didn't have anything to do with Nikos's photos. So what was it?

"I tell you what," Victoria said, sliding my workbook away from me. "Since you seem to have trouble concentrating this morning, I'll read you the questions. How's that?"

"Sure," I said, and went back to staring out the window.

If Mr. Kouropoulos had an issue with Theia Alexa, it really wasn't any of my business, of course, but Nikos had totally blown Zoe off at the table. If this argument or whatever had anything to do with how he was acting, I wanted to understand.

"Cassidy." Victoria tapped my hand with her pencil. "Are you listening?"

"Yes. Well, no. Sorry."

"Let's try again. Homer wrote that the history of the people of Zakynthos began with the arrival of what Trojan prince?" she asked.

I glanced up at her from my paper. "Huh?"

She sighed, deep and heavy, and repeated the question.

"I don't know. Hector?"

She scrubbed her hand over her face. "Well, no. Hector was *a* Trojan prince, but he's not the one I'm thinking of."

"Paris?"

"Again," Victoria said, her voice suddenly sounding very tired, "kudos for knowing the Trojan princes, but the answer to this question should be fairly obvious."

Not to me, I thought, but I didn't say it out loud.

She shook her head. "It's clear you didn't read your assignment," she said, "but you should get this if you even glanced at it. Did you glance at it?"

I chewed my lip. "Sort of."

"So you know the answer to this question would be . . . ?"

I shrugged.

Victoria sighed again. "Zakynthos, Cassidy. Homer wrote that the history of the people of Zakynthos began with the arrival of Prince *Zakynthos*. What's going on with you today?"

"I don't know," I said. "I can't think."

"It's contagious." She massaged her temples. "Go on. Get out of here. We'll continue the lesson later."

I rushed from the room before she could change her mind. Maybe Zoe's mom told her what was going on. I wanted to talk to her to find out.

Zoe wasn't in the galley. She wasn't in her room or hanging out on her favorite deck, either. I was going to check in the game room when I saw Nikos and his dad in the sitting area.

"Great," I muttered. I didn't know any way to get to the game room other than to pass through the sitting area.

Mr. Kouropoulos glanced up the moment I walked into the room. "Good afternoon, Miss Barnett."

"Good afternoon," I replied as pleasantly as I could.

"Why don't you join us?" he asked.

I eyed the door to the hallway that led to the game room and considered for half a second walking on by Nikos and his dad without stopping. But then my conscience or shoulder angel or whatever you want to call it whispered in my head (using Victoria's voice—go figure). Mr. Kouropoulos was our host on this trip. The least I could do was be polite to him. I sat on the stiff couch next to Nikos and tried not to scowl.

"Such a beautiful day," Mr. Kouropoulos said. "We couldn't have ordered better weather for our picnic on the beach."

Our picnic, he had said. I wondered if that meant he was going to join us. And if *that* meant there would be more paparazzi tagging along.

"It's perfect," I agreed.

"When we have free time," Nikos told me, "there are plenty of caves around the cove we can explore." He did one of those fakey suave grins that I hadn't seen since the first couple of days on the *Pandora*, and stretched his arm across the back of my seat—the way he had that day on the boat, coming back from Delos.

I moved away from him. "Yeah, that would be fun," I said. "I'll bet Zoe would love it."

Nikos didn't even flinch, the dog.

But Mr. Kouropoulos did. "Zoe?" he asked—and I could tell he was directing his question to Nikos, not me.

Nikos shrugged. "She tags along sometimes."

My hands curled into fists, and it took all the self-control I had not to punch him.

That's when I heard the unmistakable sound of Zoe's

little gasp behind me. I turned to see her in the doorway to the corridor. She must have just come from the game room. I was right that I would find her there. And I could guess from the way her eyes were watering that she heard the way Nikos just blew her off. Again. She rushed past us out of the room.

I waited for Nikos to go after her, but he didn't.

"If you'll excuse me," I said. "I have to go."

> *Prosperity is no just scale; adversity is the*
> *only balance to weigh friends.*
>   —**Plutarch**

I looked for Zoe everywhere. She wasn't in the galley or on any of the decks. I knew she wasn't in the game room. If she was in her own room, she wasn't answering the door. I don't know what I would have said to her if I had found her. I just didn't want her to be alone . . . although maybe that's what she wanted.

On the way to my own room, I saw Nikos on the promenade deck, staring out at the water. I stalked over to him and demanded, "What was that?"

I must have startled him because he jumped. "I didn't see you," he said.

Well, duh. I narrowed my eyes at him. "Zoe *tags along* with us?"

He hung his head. "She heard that, didn't she?"

"Probably. Yes. What were you thinking?"

"I had to say something. My dad . . ."

"Don't blame it on your dad," I snapped. "I don't know what's up with you when he's around, but you're like a different person. *You*, not him."

He mumbled something I couldn't quite understand, but the whining tone made it sound like another excuse to me.

"You know what?" I said. "Maybe it was a good thing Zoe heard what you said. Maybe it's best that she sees what you're really like. If this is the way you want to act, you don't deserve for her to like you."

"You're right," he said.

"What?"

He looked up at me and I could see the sweet, honest Nikos who had first stared at Zoe when we took pictures that day on the deck. He was the boy from the boat who was genuinely happy to see Zoe out-wakeboard him. Where was that boy just a few minutes ago when Zoe had been there to see?

"I'm not good enough for someone like her."

"But—"

"I'll see you on the beach," he said, and walked away.

I watched him go, a sinking feeling deep in my stomach. Had I just made things worse? *"Aaaaagh!"* I shouted out to the water. I didn't understand boys at all.

Victoria rushed around the corner, followed closely by Magus. "What is it? What's wrong?"

"Everything," I said.

She stopped and looked around the deck. Seeing nothing, she turned back to me. "We heard you yell. Is everything all right?"

"No!"

She gave Magus an apologetic smile. "I'm sorry. Could you excuse us for a moment?"

"Of course." He looked for a moment like he was going to add something else, but then he stepped back, and turned away.

Victoria wrapped an arm around my shoulders. "Do you want to tell me about it?"

I nodded.

We walked around the deck and I told her about what had happened in the sitting room.

"I see," she said. That's all. Just "I see."

"So what do I do?"

"This is a complicated issue, Cassidy. Sometimes the best thing you can do is to keep out of it."

"What?" I took a step back. "No. Zoe is my friend. I can't just—"

"Let it be," Victoria said. "They'll work things out."

I turned away, deflated. She didn't understand. *I* had started this mess by pushing Nikos and Zoe together. If

Zoe got hurt because of it, it was my fault. I wasn't going to just "let it be." I wasn't sure how, but I was going to figure out a way to fix the mess I'd helped to make.

Later that afternoon, Magus ferried everyone to Shipwreck Beach from the yacht. The crew had to go first to set up, and Theia Alexa had prepared a picnic lunch, so Nikos, Mr. Kouropoulos, Victoria, and I were left for the last trip.

Although Nikos and I didn't have any lines we had to remember for this shoot, we were supposed to be filmed eating, playing on the beach, and exploring the old ship that had been stranded there (which is how the beach got its name).

I knew all this, and I had seen pictures of the beach when I looked it up online, but nothing could have prepared me for actually going there. The beach was set back in a cove that looked like it could have been made by some-one scooping out the limestone cliffs with a giant shovel. On three sides, white cliffs shot straight up from the white sand beach. In front of that, the water was an incredible color of blue—turquoise along the shore, quickly deepening to cobalt.

Along the walls of the cove, water had carved several caves into the limestone. They were known as the blue caves, Victoria told me, because of the color of the water reflecting on the stone.

And there, in the center of all this natural beauty, sat the rusting hulk of the shipwreck, smack in the middle of the beach.

"They say that it was a smuggler's ship," Victoria said to me. "Imagine them being washed up here, with those cliffs all around, and no way to transport the smuggled goods out of the cove. I'm sure it's not what they expected, setting out."

I looked at Nikos and wondered if anything was ever what you expected from the beginning.

Magus managed to steer the boat straight up to the beach, as far as he dared to go without getting stuck on a sandbar. I was surprised to realize we were going to have to wade in from there. Fortunately, we were wearing our swimsuits, so it wouldn't matter if we got wet. I just didn't want Jacqueline to fuss over my hair and makeup again.

Nikos climbed down the ladder into the water and then reached up to help me down. I pulled back.

"I can do it," I said.

"I know you can," he said, and reached out again.

He looked so sad and earnest standing there, trying to keep his balance as the water sloshed around his waist, I actually felt bad for refusing. I climbed down a few steps and then allowed him to grab me around the waist and lift me down into the cool water. It was all very chivalrous and graceful. Or at least it would have been if a wave hadn't rolled in at that very moment and lifted the boat, pushing it toward us.

Nikos's mouth fell open, but he couldn't manage to make any words come out. Instead, he just grabbed me and pulled me out of the way—at the same moment that the rolling wave threw him off balance.

He lost his footing and pulled me down with him. I didn't even have time to take a breath before we both tumbled—very ungracefully—into the water.

When we popped up, coughing and sputtering, I could hear Jacqueline, somewhere on the sand behind us, exclaim, "Perfect. Just perfect. Now what am I supposed to do with her *hair*?"

I couldn't help it. I started laughing. And then so did Nikos. I don't know if he heard Jacqueline, or if he was just laughing because I was, but it didn't much matter to me. Since I snapped at him on the *Pandora*, Nikos hardly even looked at me, let alone smiled. His laughter felt like a new start. I still thought he was an idiot for what he said about Zoe, but I could tell he felt terrible about it. Maybe I should give him a chance to explain. Then I might have a better idea what we were going to do to fix it.

CJ decided that since Nikos and I were already in the water, they may as well get the shots of us playing on the beach before the lunch instead of after, as she had planned. "Let's see some enthusiasm!" she shouted. "Smiles. Big smiles."

As much fun as it was to play on the beach, it didn't take long for it to feel really awkward. I mean, everyone else was standing around watching, waiting for us to have enough good shots so they could eat. It's kind of hard to be spontaneous and have fun with that kind of pressure. I was relieved when CJ declared we were done.

After a quick touch-up by Jacqueline, who grumbled about it the entire time, I was able to sit down on the blanket where everyone was eating. For the first time, the whole crew was together, talking, laughing. Everyone except one of the camera guys, who was busy capturing it all on film. I guess this shoot was supposed to show how friendly and fun everyone was, and what a great time we all had working together. It would have been nice if we could have done it every day . . . like we did with the *When in Rome* crew.

I shook away that thought as quickly as it came. Thinking about *When in Rome* would only make me homesick again . . . and miss Logan even more.

After lunch was over and everything cleared away, some of the crew broke out a couple volleyball nets and set them up in the sand. I would have liked to play, but Jacqueline had just touched up my hair and makeup again and caught me eyeing the game. "Don't you dare," she said.

I sighed and folded my arms, watching from a distance. Nikos dropped out and came over to stand by me.

"I heard you got in trouble because of the Facebook pictures," he said. "I'm sorry about that."

"Yeah. Well, it was my fault. I forgot rule number three

thousand and eleven—the network has to approve all social media."

"Did you tell them it wasn't even your account?"

"I told them."

"And they didn't care?"

"They thought I was blowing off the rules. I swear, sometimes I think they're just waiting for a reason to be disappointed in me."

"Why don't you just tell them how that feels?"

"That's great advice," I said, "coming from the king of communication."

His face got tight, and he turned away from me.

"I'm sorry," I said, and reached for his arm. He shook me off. "Nikos . . ."

Just then, CJ announced we were done eating and that it was time to get some shots by the shipwreck. Nikos got up and walked over to the ruined boat without a word. I trudged after him.

CJ positioned us where she wanted us to stand to begin, and then worked with the camera guy to find just the right angle that would capture us, the frame of the boat, the white cliffs, and as much blue water as possible.

"I'm sorry," I told Nikos again. "I shouldn't have said that."

"It's okay," he said, even though I knew it really was not. "You were right."

"I was just being mean," I said, "because of Zoe. She's my friend. I don't want to see her get hurt."

"I know."

We watched CJ and the cameraman for a moment, and then he said, "My dad doesn't want me seeing Zoe."

"What?"

"He saw the two of us together last night, and he said I couldn't go out with her because of the arrange . . . well, just because."

"What do *you* want?"

He looked at me with sad eyes. "That doesn't always matter."

I could only nod in sympathy. I knew how true that could be.

17

I saw Zoe watching from the sky
deck as Magus shuttled us back to the yacht. We were too
far away for me to see her face, but she looked lonely, up
there by herself. The minute we docked with the yacht, I
ran to find her. I know Victoria had told me to stay out of it,
but I wanted Zoe to know how bad Nikos felt about what
had happened that morning. No sense in both of them being miserable over it.

She was gone by the time I got to the sky deck, so I
started looking in all the usual places. That's when I heard
Theia Alexa's angry voice coming from the small office on
the other side of the galley. She was yelling mostly in Greek
with a little English thrown in, so I didn't understand a lot

of what was being said, but there was no mistaking the fact that she was mad. I hoped Zoe wasn't the one in the office being yelled at, but I didn't want to knock on the door to find out.

I was debating what I should do when I recognized a couple of words in Theia Alexa's tirade—"that boy." Of course my ears perked up. The only person on the yacht I could think of who could be accurately described as *that boy* was Nikos.

My heart did a cliff dive. That did not sound good. I rushed to the door, all ready to knock, but stopped, fist midair. She sounded really angry. It might be cowardly, but I was afraid to face her when she was like that.

But what about Zoe? I still didn't even know if she was in there. The only way to find out was through that door. Unless . . . Up high along the wall was a row of long, narrow windows. If I could somehow climb up high enough, I might be able to peek inside the room.

The problem was, there was nothing to climb *on*. The only thing that came close was a brass railing about halfway up the wall, but no way of getting onto the railing and no hand grips I could use to climb up.

Unless . . . A little farther down the deck sat two deck chairs and a small cocktail table. I ran and grabbed one of the chairs and carried it back to set beneath the windows. And no, that wasn't as easy as it sounds. The chair was heavy, but I didn't want to make any noise by dragging it.

I climbed onto the chair and then stepped up from the chair to the railing, using the edge of the windowsill to pull myself up. Still, I couldn't see anything. The shutters on the other side of the glass were angled in such a way that I had to try to get up on my tiptoes to look down into the room.

Every muscle in my body strained with the effort of trying to stay balanced on that rail while holding myself close enough to the wall to peek in through the blinds. I had just about managed it when—

"What are you doing?"

I startled and lost both my grip on the window ledge and my balance on the railing. I panicked and grasped at one of the light fixtures. Which came off in my hand as I fell back. On top of Nikos.

I've tried to replay the choreography of the fall several times in my head, but it all happened so fast, I really don't know what happened. I must have let go of the fixture because I apparently grabbed Nikos's arm and I tumbled over him, pulling him right down with me onto the hard wooden deck.

We both tried to scramble to our feet, but since our arms and legs were all tangled up, we just succeeded in tumbling over each other again. Nikos's full weight ended up on top of me.

"Can't. Breathe."

"Sorry." He braced his hands on either side of my head to push himself up, pulling my hair in the process.

"Ouch!"

But he didn't apologize the second time. He was already on his feet and picking up the broken fixture. "Oh, no, no, no." And then he said some words in Greek I'm pretty sure were cuss words, the way he spit them out of his mouth.

I scrambled to my feet and grabbed his arm. "Come on!" We'd made enough noise, I was sure Theia Alexa was going to show up on the deck at any moment.

He ran with me up the deck and down a flight of stairs and into a small alcove that held a pile of round life preservers. And he was still cradling the light fixture.

"What were you doing?" he demanded.

"I was . . . looking for Zoe." It was the truth.

"My dad's going to kill me."

"For what?"

He held up the fixture. "We can't go around breaking stuff! This isn't our . . . It's not good."

"I'm sorry. I'll tell him it was my fault."

"It *was* your fault."

I couldn't believe he was getting so worked up about it. "I know. I'll pay for it. Don't worry."

That didn't seem to make him feel any better. "What were you doing up there?"

"I told you. I was looking for Zoe."

"It looked more like you were spying on Zoe."

"No, I wasn't. I don't even know if she was in that room."

Nikos shook his head. "Leave it alone, Cassidy."

I wished people would stop telling me to do that. "Leave what alone? I was just trying to help you—"

"Don't. You don't know . . . Just don't."

"Look, I'm sorry about what I said earlier."

"It's not about that."

"Then what—?"

He handed me the fixture. "Here. This is yours," he said. And then he was gone.

"I don't get it," I told Logan that night. "I found this exact light fixture online. It's less than a hundred euros to replace. Plus, it wasn't even his fault."

"Could be it's not the cost that's worrying him. His da doesn't sound like the most reasonable man."

"I guess not."

"How did you say you broke it again?" Logan asked.

I hadn't said. And I wasn't going to say. Logan would tease me forever if he knew what I'd been doing. Meddling, he called it. And he knew me well enough to know I couldn't help myself. "We were just messing around on the deck and I lost my balance," I told him. "I grabbed at it to keep from falling." At least that was the partial truth.

"Just be honest," Logan said.

My heart stopped for a second. "What?"

"Just tell his da what happened."

Oh, right. That. "Yeah. I'll tell him I broke it."

"It won't be so bad," Logan assured me. "Nothing ever is if you just tell the truth."

Travel tip: Never say anything that can be construed as challenging the honor or integrity of your host, or challenge his statements.

I finally found Zoe the next morning after breakfast. She was clearing the table and I helped her.

"Are you going to come to Paxos with us this morning?" I asked.

"I . . . must work," she said.

"I could help get your jobs done," I offered. "We don't go until about eleven and if we hurry—"

She planted the clearing tray on her hip. "I cannot."

"I could ask your mom for you. We could tell her—"

"Cassidy," she said in a sharp tone I'd never heard from her before, "I do not want to go."

I set the final spoon and fork on her tray. "Oh. Okay."

"Please excuse me," Zoe said, and left me standing at the table wondering what had just happened.

I can see the island of Paxos in the distance. Already it looks greener than a lot of the other islands we've visited so far. Lots of olive groves, Victoria says. We'll be docking there in just a couple of hours for our final shoot before we reach Corfu tomorrow.

The legend of Paxos is that it was made by
Poseidon as a getaway for his girlfriend, Amphitrite.
He supposedly struck his trident on the bottom of
Corfu and dragged the piece of land that broke off
a little farther south.

We'll get to—

Someone knocked on my door. I shut the top on my computer and rushed to open it, hoping to see Zoe standing
there. I found Magus waiting in the hallway instead.

"Oh," I said in my eloquent way. "Hi."

"Good morning, Miss Cassidy," he said. "I've been sent
to tell you that you are wanted in the salon." His deep voice
made the summons sound ominous.

My stomach sank like a bad soufflé. The fixture. I hadn't
talked to Nikos's dad about it yet, even though I had seriously planned to. As soon as I worked up the nerve.

"Oh," I said again. My mind was racing too fast to come
up with anything deeper than that. I wondered if I should
take the broken fixture with me. Or would that just make
things worse? How was I going to explain what I was doing when the thing got busted? Mr. Kouropoulos must be
plenty mad already if he had sent Magus to fetch me instead of Zoe or Victoria or Nikos or someone.

"Is everything okay?" I probed.

Magus actually looked apologetic. "Yes, miss," he said.
"Could you come with me now, please?"

I felt like a prisoner walking to the gallows as I followed Magus through the corridors and up the stairs and around the deck to the salon. My chest grew tighter with every step.

Magus stopped at the top of the stairs that led down to the salon and swept his arm forward. I swallowed hard. Whatever it was, I was going to have to face it myself.

I took each step downward slowly, deliberately, steeling myself for whatever waited for me on the other side of the door.

At the bottom of the steps, I stopped dead. I could see through the glass that CJ was in there. And Victoria. Nikos sat slumped into a chair and his dad towered over him, the scowl on his face like one of those tragedy masks. Actually, CJ's face didn't look much better. And when Victoria turned to face me, the disappointment on her face hit me smack in the chest so hard I could barely take a breath. She motioned for me to come in, and like a robot, I made myself obey.

Inside the door, it was silent. Everyone turned to look at me. Everyone but Nikos, that is.

"What's wrong?" I asked finally, my voice small.

"This"—Mr. Kouropoulos slapped a newspaper onto CJ's desk—"is what's wrong."

A newspaper? Now I was really confused. If we weren't gathered to talk about the broken fixture, then what—

I stared at the paper and my heart sank. I'll be the first

to admit it looked bad. I couldn't read the headline because it was written in Greek, but the photos accompanying the story showed Nikos and me when we had fallen onto the deck. Only it didn't look like we had just fallen. From the angle of the camera, it looked like Nikos and I were making out. In one photo, he was on top of me and it looked like my arms were wrapped around his neck. Down below the text, a photo showed Nikos fastening my necklace for me in that shop on Mykonos. There we were again on Delos, with him giving me a piggyback ride. And on Zakynthos, arms around each other, as we were just about to get toppled by that wave. But the picture that made my heart sink was of me and Nikos, sprawled on the deck again, our faces almost touching. If you didn't know what was really happening, it looked as if Nikos was about to kiss me.

"This isn't what it looks like," I said. I hated the way my voice trembled, but I was turning cold inside. It was like Spain all over again—the tabloids, the twisted situations. They could make anything look like something it wasn't, but everyone would believe the lies anyway because the pictures were "proof."

"Well, of course it isn't," Mr. Kouropoulos snapped. "But that doesn't much matter once this hits the news-stands, now does it?"

"It's not her fault, Papa," Nikos said. "Stop yelling at her."

It was the first time I had heard Nikos talk back to his dad. And probably the first time his dad had heard it, too, judging by the way his face turned all purple as he turned on Nikos. "And what were you thinking, eh? You knew the paps were out there. This was not the type of image we talked about for you."

"Papa," Nikos said, gesturing with his eyes at the rest of us.

"Well, I personally don't understand what all the fuss is about," CJ said. "You knew this girl was tabloid fodder before you signed on for this gig."

"Ex*cuse* me?" Victoria said.

CJ shrugged. "Well, it's not exactly the kind of image we'll push when we get closer to airtime, but—"

"I should say not," Victoria fumed.

I was still standing in the middle of the floor, trying to make sense of what was happening. Victoria gestured for me to sit next to her, and I sank onto the cushions gratefully.

Which is when my cell phone rang. With my mom and dad's ringtone. Perfect. If they came unglued over the Facebook photos, they were going to have dual aneurysms over this.

I handed the phone to Victoria. "Please," I told her. "I can't talk to them right now."

Victoria didn't look all that thrilled to talk to them, either, but she took a deep breath and slid the phone open. "Hello, Julia. Davidson. Yes. It appears that we have a slight problem."

• • • • •

Nikos and I both sat uncomfortably throughout the whole discussion. *If no one wanted our input*, I thought, *why did we have to be there?* It was just awkward.

Mr. Kouropoulos said he was *done* and that we were going straight to Corfu and it was *over*. CJ said she had a show to complete and two more days of shooting and if we didn't finish, we'd be in violation of our contract with the network. Mr. Kouropoulos reminded her that he was the one paying for everything, to which she responded that we still had a contract and she intended to enforce it. Victoria relayed everything to my mom and dad over the phone.

Once Mr. Kouropoulos finally calmed down, they decided we could complete the show, but he still wasn't happy about it. I escaped from the room when they started discussing whose responsibility it was to tighten security for the remainder of the cruise.

I stomped back toward my cabin, thinking about how backward everything had gotten. If the paparazzi wanted to play up a romance on board the *Pandora*, they were looking at the wrong girl. I didn't even *like* Nikos. Not in that way anyway. How come there were no pictures of him with Zoe? They were the ones who belonged together.

Speaking of Zoe, I saw her at the railing and rushed over to talk to her. When she saw me coming, she turned away.

"Zoe, let me explain."

"I think you were my friend," she said.

"I was. I am. Those pictures are not what they look—"

"It is not the pictures. You *spy* on my mother!"

Oh. She knew about that. "Look, I didn't hear anything. I was just trying to—"

She shook her head. "Go away."

"But I just wanted—"

"Please."

The shoot on Paxos was just pathetic. As long as the cameras were rolling, Nikos was all enthusiasm and smiles, talking about Poseidon and the Fifteen-Hundred-Year-Old Olive Tree! in a grove on Paxos, but between takes, he hardly even looked at me. Forget about talking.

I wanted to remind him that the paparazzi thing wasn't my fault—only that wasn't exactly true. If I hadn't been trying to spy on Theia Alexa, I wouldn't have fallen on top of him, and if I hadn't fallen on top of him, the paparazzo wouldn't have been able to get any sensational shots to misrepresent. I left him alone and felt alternately sorry for myself and really mad at everyone else.

Once we got back to the yacht, Zoe avoided me the entire rest of the evening. I finally gave up and told Victoria I didn't feel well, and went back to my room early. The only thing that kept me going was waiting for my nightly video chat with Logan. But even though I waited an hour past lights-out, he never signed in.

I couldn't sleep tonight, so I sat out on my balcony, watching the moonlight spill across the water. Its reflection floated on the surface like liquid diamonds, shimmering, shifting. It looked a lot like the reflection I saw when I sat out there just a few nights ago. Just as bright. Just as beautiful.

But it wasn't the same. We were in a different place.

Like Heraclitus said, the water is constantly moving. That means the reflection I see at this moment will be different from the one I will see in just a few seconds. It's always changing.

Just like me.

I deleted the post instead of publishing it and shut my computer and crawled into bed, feeling dramatic and hopeless and a little bit lost. I was like the moonbeam, with no control how the water would move me. Logan didn't want to talk to me. Zoe didn't want to talk to me. Nikos didn't want to talk to me. My hopes of returning to *When in Rome* were probably smashed. And there was nothing I could do about any of it.

Or was there?

I switched on the bedside lamp and pulled out Magus's book and skimmed through the pages until I found the quote I was looking for. It was from Socrates. "Let him that would move the world first move himself."

I had read that before, but I didn't know what it meant.

Now it seemed simple. If I wanted a change in fortune, I had to start with a change in myself.

I turned the light off again and lay back against the pillows.

And thought.

I found Nikos in the game room the next morning. He was sitting in front of the screen with his video game turned on, but he wasn't playing. He was just staring at the screen.

I sat next to him. "Are you okay?"

He shrugged.

"Do you know where Zoe is?" I asked.

He shook his head.

"I need to find her and tell her I'm sorry."

No response.

"Because I value her friendship."

We sat quietly for a while longer and then I turned to face him.

"She really likes you, you know. I wish you would talk to her, too."

He slid a quick look at me and then went back to staring at the screen.

"My dad . . ."

"I'm not talking about your dad. You're the one who likes her."

His ears turned red.

"Okay. I'm going to go now," I said.

And I left him to stew.

The way I figured it, some things were beyond my ability to change. I had no control over the paparazzi or Nikos or what my mom and dad thought. But I could try to mend my friendship with Zoe. That was too important to me to let it go.

> *Be as you wish to seem.*
> —Socrates

I found Zoe perched on a stool in the corner of the galley, peeling potatoes. I approached her carefully, afraid she'd run away again if I made any sudden movements. "Hi, Zoe."

She looked up from her potatoes long enough to acknowledge me and then turned back to her job.

"Please tell me you aren't still mad at me," I said.

She attacked the potato with her peeler. "No, I am not angry at you."

I was relieved to hear her say that, but it didn't take a genius to tell she was upset about *something*. I took an empty plastic food drum and turned it over like a stool. Then I scooted it close to her and sat down. "Can I help?"

She shrugged, so I grabbed another potato and a peeler that was lying on the stainless-steel counter.

"I was wrong to spy on your mom. Whatever I thought . . . it was none of my business. I disrespected your privacy and I'm sorry."

Her peeler passed over the potato in a steady rhythm. She didn't look up, but she finally said, "Thank you."

I felt so much better. Lighter. Even though I knew it was only the first step.

"I was just talking to Nikos," I said.

She peeled even harder.

"He really likes you," I ventured.

"I know."

Okay. That was good, right? I scraped the peeler along my potato a couple of times, confused. If she already knew how much he liked her, why didn't she sound happy?

"I think Nikos is afraid to say anything to you. . . ."

She held her potato and peeler still in her lap and finally looked up at me for real. "I know this. I hear Nikos and his father talking last night."

"Oh. Uh . . ." I didn't know where to go from that. Nikos must have told his dad how he really felt. That should have been a good thing.

"Nikos and I . . ." Her voice trailed off and she shook her head. "My mother . . ."

"Are you afraid you can't like Nikos because he's the boss's son? Because that's so old—"

"He is not the boss," she said. "Nikos's father . . . he is a client."

Now I was confused. Zoe's English was pretty good, but maybe she had the wrong word. Or did boss and client translate the same?

"My mother tell me, without this charter, we could lose . . ." She swallowed and blinked really fast a few times. Were those tears clinging to her eyelashes?

My stomach turned cold. "Lose what?" I asked.

She leaned closer, her eyes darting back and forth. "The *Pandora*," she whispered.

It took a minute for that to sink in. Lose the *Pandora*? "Oh," I murmured. "The *Pandora* is not his yacht."

She shook her head. "He only charter her for this trip." She was right: that made Mr. Kouropoulos a client.

I remembered the photo of Zoe's family standing on the pier when she was a baby. It all made sense now. "The *Pandora* is yours."

Zoe nodded and stared at her hands miserably. "I was not supposed to say."

"What do you mean, you could lose her?"

"It is not good time for anyone," she said quietly. "My father's investment business is bad. He loses too much money. So my parents decide for the summer season they will charter the *Pandora*. But still the money is tight. We have to release some of the crew. My mother loves to cook, so . . ."

"Wow." I shook my head, trying to adjust what I thought I knew. "But why did Mr. Kouropoulos pretend the *Pandora* was his?"

"Because he needs the publicity," Nikos said.

I whipped around on my stool to see him standing in the doorway.

"He hasn't gotten a new role in almost two years," Nikos continued. "In his business, that's like being dead. So he hoped he could use this special to keep the Kouropoulos name in the tabloids."

Now my hands went cold. "He *wanted* you in the tabloids?"

"It's cheap publicity," Nikos said.

I noticed he didn't say free.

And then it made sense to me. Why there were hordes of photographers in the big cities where everyone could see them, but none on Delos. None at the beach. "Has he been . . . paying them to follow us?"

Nikos nodded. "He says it's cheaper than hiring a publicist."

"But he seemed so angry yesterday when he talked about the pictures in the paper."

"That's because the photographers were only supposed to take flattering pictures. That was part of the deal. But then this paparazzo tried to start a scandal. He threatened to tell about the arrangement if we didn't come up with more money, but my dad just spent the last bit of money he had."

I looked from Nikos to Zoe. "And you both *knew* all this?"

"She didn't know anything!" Nikos said quickly.

"Except about the charter," Zoe said.

I shook my head. Everyone had been acting. Nikos, his dad, Theia Alexa, Zoe, the paparazzi. "Am I the only one without a part in this drama?"

"Oh, you have a part," Nikos said. "I was supposed to make it look like . . ." He coughed.

"Oh. My. Gosh." I thought of all those times he tried to be flirtatious and suave. "You were supposed to pretend you *liked* me?"

He shrugged. "You were pretty big in the tabloids for a while. My dad thought a shipboard romance might generate even more publicity."

"And you played along with it?"

"Not very well," Nikos said sheepishly. "Why do you think he kept getting mad at me?"

"I don't believe this." I slammed my potato and my peeler down on the table. I was so angry, I wanted to hit him. "What if I had liked you back? What then? And what about Zoe? How was she supposed to feel about it?"

"I didn't know Zoe when this all started," Nikos said. He looked over at her adoringly, but how was I supposed to believe him now?

"So this whole thing," I said, "was nothing but an act."

Zoe started to say something, but stopped herself.

"No. Don't stop. What were you going to say?" I asked her.

"You also act," she said.

"How?"

"Your Logan," she said. "You do not tell him how you feel."

"That's because I don't know if he . . ." But then I stopped. She was right. I was keeping secrets, too. "Okay. Fine."

"It's like a trap, isn't it?" Nikos said.

Zoe and I agreed. All three of us sat glumly for a moment, feeling sorry for ourselves.

I even felt sorry for Mr. Kouropoulos in a way. Yes, he had pretty much orchestrated the whole mess, but I understood the desperation he must have felt when he saw his career slipping away. I felt the same thing, wanting to get back to my mom and dad's show. Desperation makes you do dumb things. And now he was trapped, too.

Unless . . .

"Nikos, what's the worst thing that would happen if people knew your dad didn't own the yacht?" I asked.

"They might think he's a poser. . . ."

"But only if he was posing, right? What if he flat out told everyone about his mistake with the paparazzi and how it backfired?"

"It would be a scandal," Nikos said, starting to understand. He grinned.

"I don't understand," Zoe said.

"People hate lies," I told her, "but they love confessions.

That paparazzo guy is threatening to expose the lies. But if Nikos's dad beats them to it, there's nothing to expose. People will forgive him because he has admitted what he did wrong."

"And you can't buy that kind of publicity," Nikos added.

"Right," I said. "But it has to be sincere. No more lies. Otherwise, he just builds himself another trap."

"How you know so much about this?" Zoe asked.

"I've gone the confession route before," I told her. "Plus, Logan's dad is our executive producer. He lives for ratings. He would absolutely eat this up. . . ." I let the words trail off and glanced at the clock.

"What's wrong?" Nikos asked.

"Nothing." I jumped down from the stool. "You go talk to your dad. I have an idea."

Life must be lived as a play.
—**Plato**

It was nearly midnight in New Guinea by the time I was able to set up the call, but my mom and dad and Cavin all crowded around the screen, looking very much awake. I was hoping I'd see Logan, too, but this was a business teleconference. Not his kind of thing.

"I'm just so proud," Cavin said. "Ye've learnt the publicity game very quickly, Cass."

"I've had a good teacher."

Cavin always said to "strike while the iron was hot." As soon as Mr. Kouropoulos's confession hit the airwaves, everyone on the yacht would be getting their fifteen minutes of fame, whether they liked it or not. The best way to capitalize on that fame was to be prepared with the next venture while name recognition was at its peak.

"Tell yer parents what ye've come up with," Cavin said.

"You know how some musicians can play by ear?" I asked. "Well, Theia Alexa cooks by heart. While she's been sailing around with her charters, she's been discovering regional foods and re-creating them in her kitchen. Tell me that doesn't sound like a great premise for a cooking show."

Even my mom, *When in Rome*'s dedicated foodie, sounded impressed. "It's a wonderful idea. But how is she on camera?"

"Thanks to CJ and the crew," Cavin said, "I've just seen an audition tape this afternoon. She's great. Corporate's already on board."

"I hoped maybe you could come meet us in Corfu and tape an episode with her," I said. "You know, a little cross-promotion? Mr. Kouropoulos has already agreed to let them use his name as a cosponsor, and he'd be doing some cameos, too."

"My, you have been busy," Mom said.

"Dad?" I asked. "You haven't said anything."

He blinked at the webcam. "That's because I'm speechless. Who are you and what did you do with my daughter?"

● ● ● ● ●

I invited Mr. Kouropoulos, Theia Alexa, and CJ into the chat, and we spent the rest of the time working out the details of our next move. I have to give Mr. Kouropoulos credit; he warmed up to the confession idea pretty quickly. It's never easy to admit when you're wrong, but I guess it's even harder to *stay* wrong.

Theia Alexa still looked shocked. She kept hugging me and about anyone else within arm's length all day. I think that was a pretty good indication she was happy about the idea of her own cooking show.

CJ was as cool and professional as ever, calmly ditching our last at-sea day of filming (I mean, really, how many onboard B-roll shots did they need?) so she could shoot Theia Alexa's audition tape and some publicity stills to accompany Mr. Kouropoulos's comeback.

We'd been right about the fifteen minutes. He'd had four scripts sent over to read since he shared his story on the local news. He showed a rare glimpse at his human side, coming clean about how he planned to use his son (tween heartthrob, the papers said) to resurrect his career. The papers went on to report how the newly humbled Mr. Kouropoulos would be cosponsoring a new cooking show, *Greek by Heart,* starring Alexa Papadakis, and how Davidson and Julia Barnett of *When in Rome* fame would be on hand for the launching of this new venture.

All's well that ends well, right? At least that's what I was trying to remind myself when we left the yacht in Corfu. As happy as I was about how everything turned out, I was sad to see the adventure come to an end.

Zoe had promised we could video chat, once she got her computer at home set up. She and Nikos discovered they live within ten blocks of each other. How's that for fortune? He promised to go watch her next swim competition.

Logan, I discovered, had dropped his computer while they were in New Guinea. That's why he didn't sign in to our chat that last night. When I pressed him to make sure it wasn't about the tabloid pictures, he asked me, "What pictures?"

I told him to never mind.

Mom and Dad flew back with me to Ohio, but they could stay for only a couple of days before they had to leave again. The rest of the crew was still waiting for them to finish the episode in New Guinea. They promised we would talk more about *When in Rome* when they got back.

Until then, they enrolled me in school in Ohio.

I start tomorrow.

I haven't given up hope that I'll return to the show. I figure if I can stage a comeback for Constantine Kouropoulos, I can figure out one for myself.

You never know when fortunes can change.

Epilogue

The last time I was at a Halloween party, I dressed as a fairy princess, complete with gossamer wings and a wand that lit up. It was a network function, and I couldn't wait to go so I could show off my costume. I was seven. There were no other kids at the party.

After that, Halloween lost its mystique for me. What was the point? Mom and Dad never let me eat much candy, so trick-or-treating was a waste of time. I didn't know any kids my age, so parties were no fun. And usually, when the date rolled around, we weren't even in a country that celebrated Halloween. After a while, I became a kind of Halloween Scrooge.

So I was unexpectedly excited when Charlene Jackman—

the most popular girl at Buckeye Hills Middle School—invited me to her house for a costume party.

"What do they *do* at a costume party?" Logan wanted to know when we video chatted after the invitation.

"I don't know," I said. "Dress up. Eat. Listen to music."

"Sounds great," he said sarcastically.

"Don't spoil it for me," I said. "This is the first time one of them has let me into their circle."

"A costume party is a circle?"

"I'm going to disconnect."

He made a pouty face. "I'm sorry."

"You don't get it," I told him. "When I came back to Ohio the first time, I enrolled in school just before the school year started. I went to the open house and everything. Then I got sent to Greece."

"And after your adventure in Greece . . ."

"The press wouldn't leave me alone. I didn't ask them to follow me to school on my first day back but—"

"Ha!" Logan laughed. "I forgot they did that. Police had to escort them off school property, yeah?"

"It wasn't funny. Everyone thought I was stuck-up, even though I totally tried to make friends with them. Gramma even made cookies for me to share at lunch."

"She did not."

I drew my finger in an *X* over my heart. "I swear."

"Well, did it work?"

"Not even." I frowned, remembering. "Before I could pass them out, Tyler Smitty grabbed the sack from me and started a peanut-butter-cookie fight in the cafeteria."

Logan laughed again. "You never told me that."

"It's not something I want to remember. One of the girls in my grade is allergic to peanuts. Her face swelled up and they had to call the paramedics because she couldn't breathe. After that, everyone started calling me *la chica nutta*."

He laughed out loud, wiping his eyes with the back of his hand.

"I really am going to disconnect," I warned him.

"I hafta go anyway," Logan said, still chuckling. "Da says my time's up. Have fun at your party, *chica nutta*."

Gramma offered to make me a costume for the party. I wanted to go as Lady Gaga. I showed Gramma some pictures to give her costume ideas, and I thought she was going to have a stroke. She decided I would go as Little Bo Peep instead. I am not kidding. She made me a costume complete with ruffled pantaloons and a stuffed lamb and a shepherd's crook (tied with a blue satin bow).

"You look adorable!" she gushed as she tied the matching ribbon that held on my hat.

Adorable. Just what I did not want to be. But what was I going to do? I love my gramma. She just spent all week in her sewing room making me the costume. I wasn't about to hurt her feelings.

I went as Bo Peep.

I got cold feet when Gramma went to drop me off in front of Charlene's house. Everyone else walking up to Charlene's front door was dressed as something scary. Like a zombie, or a wolfman, or a ghost. No one was adorable.

"Can you drive around the block?" I begged.

She sighed a long, you're-killing-me sigh, but she did the drive-around anyway.

"The only way you won't fit in is if *you* think you don't you fit in," she told me. I was going to argue that it didn't matter what I thought; Bo Peep and Zombies were diametrically opposed. But then she looked so sad and hopeful, and I was afraid she'd feel bad for not making me a more terrifying costume, so I decided to accept my humiliation and go to the party.

I said good-bye to Gramma, and she promised to come pick me up at nine.

When I rang the bell, Charlene was already waiting at her door. "Cute costume," she told me. Emphasis on *cute*. I personally think she smirked when she said that, but it could have been my imagination. She showed me back to the great room where everyone else—in their scary, bloody, normal costumes—were already dancing, talking, eating, and generally having fun.

I could feel all eyes on me as I tried to work my way as inconspicuously as possible to the other end of the room where I saw an empty spot on the couch. In case you're wondering, it's pretty hard to be inconspicuous in a hoop-skirt that keeps hitting everyone's legs as you pass.

By the time I made it over to the couch, the spot was taken. I turned to make my way back across the room and hit Rodney Elton in the head with the crook of my staff. He dropped his plate, and I bent to help him pick it up.

Never bend over in a hoopskirt.

I never thought I'd say I was grateful for ruffled panta-loons, but at that moment, I truly was.

With as much dignity as I could fake, I skirted the rest of the group and left the party. I'm pretty sure I could hear their laughter behind me as I started the two-mile walk back to Gramma's.

In case you're wondering, two miles is a long way to walk, dressed as Bo Peep. But it gives you a long time to wallow in self-pity. And then, when you get over yourself, to think. I remembered once, when we were on a flight with those personal entertainment screens, I watched that old Reese Witherspoon movie where the sorority girl goes to Harvard Law School. The main character got invited to a costume party and went dressed as a bunny, with ears and cottony tail and everything.

Just like me, she found herself in a room filled with

other students, all wearing regular clothes and laughing at her, trying to make her feel small.

In the movie, that party was a turning point for her character. She had to decide that she really wanted to stay at Harvard, and that she was willing to work as hard as she could to prove she belonged there.

I decided if Reese Witherspoon could do it, so could I. I was going to show everyone I was smart enough and tough enough and *regular* enough to be accepted at Buckeye Hills.

I actually got excited about it. It was like a crusade.

At school on Monday, I held my head high and laughed along with anyone who called me *chica nutta*, or who baaaa-ed as I walked by. I made an effort to learn their names so I could say hi to them next time we passed.

At lunch, I walked right over and plopped my tray down on Charlene's table and sat with the popular girls.

"I'm sorry I had to leave your party early on Saturday," I told her. "But I lost my sheep and I didn't know where to find them."

I swear, Becki Daniels thought I was serious for a moment before Charlene started laughing.

It wasn't much, but it was a chip at the social ice. I ate lunch with them the rest of the week.

Which is why, when I got the call from the network, I actually hesitated.

"Yer still trending in the social media," Cavin told me. "In terms of ratings potential, that's huge."

I twisted the telephone cord around my fingers (yes, Gramma still had one of those phones with the long, curly cords). "That's cool."

"Cool?" he scoffed. "Darlin', it's phenomenal. It took some doin', but I've come up with funding for a new assignment for you."

My face went numb. "Assignment?"

"Yes. Now I know yer mum and dad are on their way to see you, but I convinced them to let me tell you the news."

"What news?"

"The network wants to run spots on the kids' stations, corresponding with the *When in Rome* episodes. Tie-ins, you could say."

I nodded as if he could hear my head move on the other end of the line.

"Do ye hear what I'm sayin', Cass? They want you to do the spots on location. Ye'll be traveling with the show again—starting in Costa Rica!"

I sank into Grampa's old La-Z-Boy chair. That was what I wanted, right? To be back with the show. To be with Logan.

But . . .

Would it seem like I was running away if I left school again? I'd made all those plans. I actually kind of wanted to see if I could pull off a watch-me-rock comeback.

On the other hand . . .

"Hello? Are ye there, Cass?"

I sat up straight. "Yes, I'm here."

"So what do ye think? Do ye want to do the spots or not?"

"I don't know," I said. "I've got a lot going on at school."

"Are ye bein' straight with me? Stop joshin' around. Just say yes and be done with it."

"All right. I'll say yes . . . on one condition."

He laughed. "Oh, so we're makin' conditions now, are we? How quickly fame goes to the head. All right, darlin', what is it?"

I took a deep breath and smiled. Okay, so this wasn't the turning point I'd been planning, but it could be an even better one.

"I'll do the spots," I told Cavin.

"Yes?"

"As long as Logan does them with me."

ISBN: 978-0-14-241816-1

Cassidy is thrilled when the time comes for her and Logan to start filming publicity spots for their parents' TV show in Costa Rica. But there's a damper on her sunshiny outlook when she discovers that someone hacked into her blog and is posting some pretty negative things—jeopardizing her whole role on the show. Can Cassidy enlist Logan's help and figure out what's going on—before it's lights out for Lights, Camera, Cassidy?

Get Hooked
ON THESE OTHER
FABULOUS
Girl Series!

Lucy B. Parker: Girl vs. Superstar
By Robin Palmer
AVAILABLE NOW!

Forever Four
By Elizabeth Cody Kimmel
AVAILABLE NOW!

Lights, Camera, Cassidy: Episode 1: Celebrity
By Linda Gerber
Coming Soon! 3/15/2012

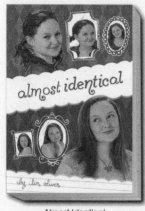

Almost Identical
By Lin Oliver
Coming Soon! 6/28/2012

Check out sample chapters at
http://tinyurl.com/penguingirlsampler